Antiphony

Laila Stien

Antiphony

A Novel

Tr. John Weinstock

Nordic Studies Press

An earlier version of this book was published in Norwegian as Vekselsang,
Copyright © Tiden Norsk Forlag 1997. [All rights reserved.]

Cover art by Elina Helander-Renvall

This translation has been published with the
financial support of NORLA.

For Ellen Anna

Contents

The Blue Room

Everything would have been easier had I been the sort that kept quiet. Kept things to myself, didn't chatter away. It was my own trap I had fallen into; I had no one to blame. I thought, where I sat. The bus kept a steady pace. The road was straight. Wide and fine, with a yellow stripe down the middle. We had emerged into open terrain, had an unobstructed view in all directions after having wandered and wound our way higher and higher up from the narrow chasm that formed the passage from the low country to the high plateau. A mountain split right in two. In the Precambrian or whenever it might have been. Not attractive in any case – dark and narrow.

A good deal better up on top. Fiery red sun over autumn leaves and heather. Although I was sitting the whole time with the unpleasant feeling of having gotten involved, gotten lost, not only in an unnecessary, but an absolutely distasteful errand. And just because I had been so loose-mouthed!

I let myself be provoked, that's the way it is. Let myself be heckled and controlled.

And now I had ended up here. Because my so-called good friend and colleague had suggested a certain lack in me. Initiative, she had called it. Referring no doubt to various things.

Initiative!

It was beautiful. That much was undebatable. Not that picturesque surroundings have usually meant so much to me, but it made a certain impression. Just now it did. If I hadn't had fellow passengers, I would certainly have started to bawl out that Ulf Lundell song, "I'm happiest out in the open ..." and so on.

But I wasn't alone. And I was probably strange enough as it was. A couple of those who got on one or two stops after the airport had stared rather openly. I was clearly different, without entirely being able to say why. The youngest of them also had a windbreaker. Not all that different from mine. But anyway – I found out that it was a bad sign. It was now somehow I who had come to take a close look at things. Although – from the very first fateful day when it had been decided, leave obtained and all that, I had taken everything as bad signs: the weather, the traffic jam, a run in a stocking, whatever.

"They're gone now. Nearly all of them are gone. It was worst with my kind-hearted husband who was buried in the dark.

He should have thought about it, the minister, but he probably doesn't understand, spoke way too long.

And all the eulogies that were supposed to be read. They surely didn't need to interpret everything, in wintertime.

My good, hard-working husband – and then to be buried in darkness!"

She turns her head slowly toward the window, as if to bring in light. Her hair is almost not gray, lies dark and smooth around her face, which is hollowed, the features in a way too large, there is so little filling it out, everything becomes distinct.

They say she was the beauty in the village, and that she kept them waiting, the suitors, several at a time. That sort of thing gave status. That sort of thing still gives status. It would have been adequate if she had been only half as proud, her sister is supposed to have said. The one who had to be content with the first one that came along. With a crooked nose and large feet she couldn't expect just anybody.

"Thanks for coming. And God's blessing."

She stretches out her hand, lays it over mine. Bony and white, but warm. For a short while she keeps her hand there. Then takes it back slowly, lets it fall down along her side, rest against the white bedding. Everything is white here. Broken only by a framed picture in small format, it hangs over the headboard, she cannot see it. It depicts Moses on Mount Nebo. He is looking out over the promised land.

The curtains are soft. The whole room is drained of color, subdued. So different from the huge room she has lived in, open sky, abundant.

"Thanks," she says one more time.

I pass a willow grove on the way home. The colors sucked away there too. A white willow grove under a cobalt sky.

A few days pass before I am there again. I think I mustn't be too eager. One nurse had stared at me. "Family?" she had asked. "No, I said." Let it go at that. Stingy or defiant or impolite.

In that case we were both impolite.

She is singing as I step in. In a little, broken voice and without a hymnal she is singing. It is a well-known hymn, so I know how the words go. *Then take my hands …*

I remain standing at the door until she is finished. She has noticed that I am there, but doesn't let herself be distracted. Now she turns her face toward me, a silent movement on the pillow.

I say Good Morning and she answers May God grant that the day be good, as is the custom.

"Oh, you came," she adds.

I tell about the weather and whom I saw on the way.

"It's a busy time," she says.

She turns to look toward the window, which is placed so high on the wall that nothing outside can reach her, other than the blue light. Perhaps that is enough.

I say that yes, that's right, busy now, so much has to be taken care of.

"They start too late. We started earlier. Long before Easter we had everything ready. He was a clever and hard-working man, my husband, we didn't lack anything … Do you know that he built sleighs?"

"Yes, I know that."

"The best sleighs made in these parts."

"They say so."

"He had a quiet nature, and God had blessed him with a great capacity for work, he did everything the way it was supposed to be done."

She has told this before, that they came from far away and asked for his sleighs. This was more than unusual. Such work was mostly for the farmers living here or for those on the other side of the border. The Finns have always been good sleigh makers. But it was his sleighs everyone here wanted, with the right curve, so steady that you couldn't tip them over if you moved and rocked all you were man enough to. He could be away for days looking for raw material. Used only the best.

"Yes, she sighs, – both skill and capacity for work, that he had. Success with reindeer too. We had a good life … And he was at peace when he went. Saved and dearly bought and baptized for salvation."

Was he at peace? There are many who doubt that, according to what I have understood. Some even think they have met his restless soul where it happened.

"They are gone now. All are gone. Resting in peace, in Jesus' name."

She dozes off. Isn't able to speak very long at a time. But I wait. Know that when she opens her eyes again, she will fumble. Now she has shut me out. For a moment she has gone into another room. I don't know which one. I don't have the qualifications to know how it is there, either. Even though she has talked about it.

The wolves she has talked a lot about. But I can't manage to picture them. The only ones I know walk around in a tramped down circle along the fence in a narrow enclosure.

Her wolves are different. They have teeth and come in packs. She is the fence, the one who stops them, the one who forces them back. With fire and *yoik*[1] she constrains them. It is the fire she speaks about. She never mentions the other thing. I have it from others that she was a good yoiker. Before she was saved.

This face in the reflection of the fire is the only one I manage to see. Because the skin is still young, the hair black, and since I can surely always manage to light a fire, one of the few skills I have acquired. I even start one in the shelter of the trees, where there are trees, don't do it in open, drafty places like those they laugh at.

Yes, just that I manage to see: The young, strong face, and the flames that lap up toward the sky.

She has talked about the time of her youth, about keeping watch and the drudgery. In bad winters it was impossible to keep the herd together, there wasn't enough food, the reindeer had to be released, to go free – and become quarry both for wolves and two-legged predators.

Rough weather she had spoken about. What it's like to be forced to lie down by a severe storm. Lie flat against the ground and keep stable. While the storm blows, like a stern chastiser, like a righteous God, one that punishes the disobedient. They put up with it, they expected it. The calm too, afterwards. After the frightened herd had been gathered.

She has told a lot, but the suitors she hasn't mentioned. It is the others who have done that. The worn out niece, goddaughter and namesake, the one I usually visit. It is as if she livens up when she gets to talk about her aunt. As if something else also falls to her lot. She has described the chests full of silk shawls. In detail she has described them, though it is impossible she could have seen them.

---

1. Sami chant/song.

Made up from dreams and evoked in memory and long conversations in the evenings they have become more and more real. Red, yellow and green patterned shawls. Smooth against the fingertips, shiny. But sent back. Laid in the sleigh and driven back in raging showers of loose snow and scorned oaths.

None of this did she tell me. Only about him did she speak, the best one. Who rests in peace in Jesus' name.

"Are you still here?"

"Yes."

"You are a good person. No one can hate a person like you."

I don't know anything to answer.

"I see increasing sleep over your head, are you tired?"

"A little, perhaps."

"It is warm."

"Do you want me to open the window?"

"If you could be so kind."

The nurse is in a really good humor, smiles and says it is nice of me to come, there aren't so many –

"It is a busy time," I say.

She nods. Takes the empty coffee cup on the night table with her.

"Have you seen my goddaughter? Do you know whether they have gotten hold of meat? Did they get it hung up?"

I say I have been there, but didn't notice whether anything was hanging under the ridge of the roof. Maybe it was, maybe not.

"They wait too long. The flies come before it is dry."

"I guess there is so much to do."

"I suppose."

I ask whether she has slept. You never know, she answers, the dreams are the same ones.

I ask whether she hurts. No, a little bit. They are nice, she says, help her with that too, help her with everything, may God reward them.

They call it the Disease that eats. She knows too that it can take time. So strangely fated, those who are young and need time, don't get it.

"I am fortunate. No one is afraid of me. I get food."

I nod. Know it. They were afraid before. Turned away.

"My father was alone. In the tent entirely alone."

This is one of those things she tortures herself with. I interrupt before she begins to cry, but am not completely certain whom I am protecting.

"That's quite a freeze we're having during the day," I say.

It is quiet for a while.

"No problem as long as the snow remains," she says, calmly.

A freeze while the ground is still bare I have heard about. Ice-covered pastures. Hooves that bleed from scratching in the ice. Herds wild with hunger – scattered to the four winds.

"No problem, she repeats.

The perspective no longer surprises me. So I have learned: that people freeze their limbs off, come home from the mountains without a nose and frostbitten to the point of being unrecognizable, is subordinate to everything else – that the snow is soft enough, the moss accessible, the reindeer well fed.

No problem.

"Have you heard from your relatives? Your parents – are they healthy?"

"Yes, they are healthy and active."

"That is a good gift, health is more valuable than gold, my father …"

Then we are there again. And it was me, it was my presence –

Afterwards she dozes off. But squirms, whimpers. Tiny pearls of sweat come out on her forehead.

A nurse, a young man I haven't seen before, asks me to go. Time for medicine.

"What is it she gets?"

"Petidin."

"Is there anything stronger … later on?"

"Yes, sure."

The room I rent is small and cozy. With an electric radiator under the window and an extra space heater it is no problem keeping it warm. The laptop PC lies unopened in a plastic bag. I am not writing much, just taking notes by hand. For the most part I lie in bed and stare at the ceiling. It has something to do with it almost becoming too much.

I hope he is right – that they can keep her pain free. Although pain free –

She prefers to talk about the joys. The good part of being saved. She brings that up every time. Without being insistent, without requiring confession, response. Entirely without gestures and with her eyes resting on a point outside the room or inside herself she shares her most important truth with me – that all good and complete gifts come from above, from the father of light, with whom there is no change or shifting shadow.

This she says.

It is the others who tell me about the shadows.

Her daughter she refers to as a child of God, light and mild as her father, an angel. And dexterous and handy, helped her mother out from the time she was little. Twelve-years-old she was self-sufficient in everything that had to do with food and clothing. Everything except slaughtering. Father took care of that. Mother in a pinch. The hired hands were not always there. She sewed for them all before she was confirmed. Stripped bark, boiled lye, scraped hides, and tanned and sewed. They say no one was in their living room, or tent during summer, without the young girl sitting with work in her hands. If it wasn't a needle and sinew thread, then it was the scraping board in her lap, the bark stripper in her strong fists. A blister or two was nothing she concerned herself with, she could scrape five hides in one day, or twenty pair of lower leg skins. When they got a sewing machine, she wasn't to be curbed. Her father, even though he was as rich as a lake, couldn't manage to keep her in cloth. He bartered for whatever he could get hold of in the market, and still it was not enough.

She sewed for her aunt too – the aunt with the crooked nose and ever pregnant. She gave birth yearly, one boy and girl after the other, though she was so unpleasant and not very nice.

"My sister had many children," she can suddenly say, when she lies there and I think she is napping.

"My sister was, when you get right down to it, a good person," she can add, as if she is reading my thoughts, knows what I have heard.

The angel sewed for them all. Didn't spare herself. Sewed constantly, as if there was no time to lose.

I hang my down jacket over a chair back, take my cap off and comb my hair with my fingers. The frost on the forelock melted as soon as I came in, I feel my damp hair against my forehead. I wipe away the dampness, above my mouth too.

"You have long ears, you will have a long life."

She looks at me. I am uncertain whether it is serious or a joke. She appears alert.

"My goddaughter was just here. She brought doughnuts, help yourself."

She points to the bag on the night table. I say thanks and help myself.

So she finally found time, the busy one.

If there isn't exactly color to detect in her old face, then there is a new sort of luster, something that is smoothed out.

"My namesake thinks about everyone."

"She does."

"Do you know her?"

"Yes."

"Poor goddaughter, she has many worries."

"She sure does."

"When the children are small they trample on your lap. When they get big they trample on your heart."

I don't know much about that sort of thing, but assume she is right, I nod.

"That's the way it is," she adds. "That's the way it is. Often."

She closes her eyes. I take it as a sign and shut up.

When she opens her eyes, she asks whether I can read to her. It isn't that she can't see, but it is good to hear someone read.

I glance at the well-used book. "But I …"

"There is one more, in the drawer."

I open it and find one in Norwegian.

"What would you like me to read?"

"God's word."

I open up at random. It is the apostle Paul's letter to the Romans about the good we want, but don't do and the evil we don't want, but nevertheless do:

… In my inmost self I delight in the law of God, but I perceive that there is in my bodily members a different law, fighting against the law that my reason approves and making me a prisoner under the law that is in my members, the law of sin. Miserable creature that I am, who is there to rescue me out of this body doomed to death? God alone, through Jesus Christ our Lord! Thanks be to God! In a word then, I myself, subject to God's law as a rational being, am yet, in my unspiritual nature, a slave to the law of sin.

That far I read. Either she is tired after two visits, or she has found peace in the redeeming thought about the weakness of the flesh.

She falls asleep.

It's quite light in the afternoon now. The sun is creeping steadily higher, beginning to warm up little by little, at any rate in the middle of the day. I pull my cap well down over my ears, my long ears! She has many words of wisdom, my friend. She became concerned when she heard that I had recently begun to drink coffee, that it was something I had started up here.

"It could happen that you won't get married," she said then, and shook her head.

I find a pretext to go into the store on the way home. Home? Yes. I live here. Here is where I live. It was supposed to be two months. Now it has turned into five. After four weeks I knew everything, discerned everything. Then I began to understand less. Now I know nothing, and the PC lies in a plastic bag.

I buy vacuum-packed sausages, a bag of freeze-dried potatoes, the Finnmark Daily and a milk chocolate bar. The newspaper has a first page article about resource management in Finnmark.

On the bulletin board in the store it says that the village cinema will show Pulp Fiction next Wednesday.

Two snowmobiles start up simultaneously. One is an Arctic Cat. The other is a Lynx. I know the brands now. To begin with they were red, black, yellow. Now they have names. And horsepower. Many and fast.

The boys disappear in kicked-up snow and exhaust.

He was busy, that boy too, the one she talked about one of the first days. Son of another niece. A fine boy, and helpful. He'd stopped at home for gasoline, didn't have time to eat, didn't have time to change into dry footwear. He was so busy. As they all are, who are on their way to their place of death.

The plastic bag crunches in the cold. It squeaks under the soles of the feet, the snow dry as flour.

It is pretty with the smoke from the chimneys going straight up, like glimmering columns, with a play of colors in the air particles.

It is pretty, but I don't say that to anyone. Am afraid it sounds stupid.

The biting wind is sharp over the bridge. The river runs swift a bit further up, there are breaks in the ice all winter long. Along the bank the ice has been pressed up by the current below, packed together, flakes of brittle ice stand edgeways like shining, mobile sculptures. In roughly the middle the river is safe and passable, with a staked-out snowmobile trail. Though there are tracks everywhere, from bank to bank, both over pack ice and channel.

A man well along in years comes toward me on a kick sled. He curls together against the frosty, biting wind, squeezes on the handgrips, kicks forward with all his might. He has on the full trappings – moccasins and skin stockings, but no reindeer jacket. The usual Sami jacket, perhaps two, he is blue in the nose, but he has been out many a winter day before. He is very, very old, I can see that when he comes up alongside. But whether he has long ears, is not easy to know, he has a leather cap tied well under his chin. With intense energy he kicks forward.

"The time for my passing is at hand," I remember she said the very first time. I was visiting her together with her goddaughter. Just that she has forgotten, how it started. Now I am someone who comes, at regular intervals I come.

She said something else strange one time. She said: "Where there is no wound, the blood doesn't run."

I am not sure I understood it.

I walk on in this landscape outside of time.

She has had a restless night, she has cried. They say I can go in anyway.

The smoothness is gone, her glance twisted.

She mumbles. She is sweaty. Her hair lies in thin bands over her forehead, along the ears. I say Hello, but she doesn't hear, I greet her again, but don't get a response, she doesn't see me, is lost in mumbling and sweat. Something grabs hold of me, takes my breath away, I step aside.

I am disconnected in the waiting room, hear it myself, the voice shrieks: "But give her something then!"

The nurse says it is not pain, she has gotten what there is to get.

"What is it?" I want to know.

"Sit here and wait," she says, friendly, touches my arm lightly and goes.

She is back after a few minutes.

"Now you can go in."

The nurse has combed her hair backwards, cooled her face, with a wrung-out washcloth presumably. I want to run back and thank her, but think twice.

She lies completely still. Her hands on one another over her chest, but not clasped.

She recognizes me, says hello, speaks. Speaks in a new, monotone voice, it is hers, at the same time it isn't.

"All flesh is like grass, and all its glory like the flowers in the field."

The words come slowly. The last word like a sigh.

This day I regret that I came. Feel that in a way I have snuck in. Don't know how close I am allowed to be to her sorrow.

But since I came, I sit. At the edge of the chair. Wait for someone to touch me on the shoulder, toss me out.

She has opened up, several times, but I haven't felt guilty until now. Except that one time, when she asked about my parents, whether they were healthy. Then I felt it. That I'd brought something with me.

Her whole landscape she has opened up for me. Part of it I have been able to step into. Other things have remained there – outside. Movements I wasn't able to follow, migratory routes between seasons, navigation by mountaintops and rivers with long names. Harness off, harness on, let loose and surround, drive forward. Two good herders were enough for a tame herd. Then the dogs knew what they had to do. The others came behind with the string of reindeer and sleds tied together. Packs in the fall. *That* was heavy, many miles to walk. But the spring move on hard snow – easy as the wind!

Sometimes she remembers it differently: Poor snow crust, weak animals after a winter on ice-covered pasture, dogs that succumb, draft reindeer that don't budge, long nights that don't help. When dawn comes, they have hardly gone farther than the distance you can hear a dog baying.

"He was in front, my husband, so steady on skis."

Steady in every respect, according to what I've understood. Steady in his faith.

Yet she is anguished.

No one comes and tosses me out.

I take the book and read, unasked. There is, at any rate, no one who can do this. I don't look, don't know what to look for, I read where the book opens:

For this is my Father's will that everyone, who sees the Son and believes in him, shall have eternal life, and that I shall resurrect him on the day of judgment.

"Thanks," she mumbles, "thanks, and God our heavenly father's blessing be over you."

She stretches out a hand, but doesn't find me. I come toward her.

That they had this child was something everyone was delighted with, didn't begrudge them, they had waited so long. They had everything else: Fine clothing, harnesses so painstakingly made that the eyes that saw them became dizzy. Full casks of salted whitefish, fat dried meat, more than it was possible to devour, tent canvas and blankets of the best sort, nothing wind worn or torn. And outside the timber house: Roof-high piles of dry winter wood, a large box of birch bark and twigs. Everything in obvious order. Always enough fuel, enough food. Food for everyone who came. The sister's kids came often, the crooked nose, little-too-snappish sister. They came and stayed for many days. It wasn't far to go home, they could see the smoke. Nevertheless they stayed.

After the little angel was born, they came more and more often, and stayed even longer. They were totally changed at their aunt's, helped out, carried in wood, carried in water, carried brimming buckets from the river, knocked holes in the ice during the winter, dipped and carried.

Back home again, they turned around, became stubborn and slow to obey. She said it once, the goddaughter – the oldest of the unpredictable children of the aunt, that light must be implanted in children, and it is bad for those who have no light to implant.

Was she speaking about her mother? Or about herself?

Both, perhaps.

The angel was everyone's pet. The older cousins came and came. Played with their cousin and did grown-up jobs alternately. Until their mother came for them, got hold of them and made them come home for other water buckets, more chores.

It was the darkest part of winter when she was born. He nearly lamed the draft reindeer, he who was finally going to become a father. The heavy-footed sister-in-law was not at home, she had gone with her husband far into the east mountains to pick up two young bucks that had strayed into another herd. They had just arrived, were sitting in the reindeer sleighs talking with the herders when he came in a rush like a wild animal through the loose snow and into the grazing herd. Ten to twelve animals were frightened into flight and had to be brought in again by dogs. He panted and flailed, didn't manage to say much, nor was it necessary. She didn't delay, got the draft reindeer turned around and set out after her brother-in-law at a speed so wild that people who had seen them through the thick, fine snow just as they stormed over the river ice, said that it was a miracle of God that all went well. In the twilight they could have hurt both themselves and the reindeer.

But they made it.

When the water had boiled and the knife had been cleansed in the embers, he was chased out behind the logging road, the father-to-be. There he sat on his knees in the snow and fed the draft reindeer that had nearly been driven to death with moss from a gunnysack he had alongside him, while he listened and waited and bit his lower lip so the blood ran.

Inside it couldn't have gone better, even though she was advanced in age, she who was going to become a mother for the very first time.

Yes, – everyone was happy. No one begrudged them this. During the baptism at Easter it was absolutely crowded in church. Eight children were baptized, but none was made such a fuss over as theirs. No one had more godparents or finer gifts. No one with so much heart-felt blessing on the way toward a good and truthful life according to His will. There was only one who said that he had sinned the day his daughter was born. Only a single one who hinted that a hymn probably would have been more fitting. Everyone knew that he had yoiked that day. Yoiked both his wife and the mountains where he had gotten her almost ten years earlier, yoiked loud and long, the Christian man.

I sit longer than usual that day. Every time I make a sign of getting up, she makes a little movement with her arm as if she wants to grasp, hold me back. Or she breaks the silence, holds my attention, forces me to listen. There is nothing agitated about it, nor does it seem contrived, it is just something that happens, something that comes in and preserves the moment the way we both want it, something that gets my muscles to relax so that I glide back into the seat, rest against the chair back. She lies calm and breathes without a sound. The bad from a little while ago has been driven away. So it can seem, but she says:

"It is a dead faith that doesn't bear the fruit of the faith, but the fruit of death."

The words come slowly, from her new unaccented voice.

I ask what she means, but she has said what she wanted.

She asks for water, and I draw from the faucet, cold, fresh water. Hold her head up while she drinks.

"It's hard to speak a foreign language," she says after a while. I don't deny it. Know that it's that way, also when it is not noticed. On her you hardly notice it. She is steady in her foreign language. Steadier than most. Because she's never been afraid of people, she told me the first time. Because she didn't just stay with her own people during the long summers at the coast, but kept company with everyone, she found friends and was with them in many a thing. There was just one thing she couldn't bring herself to do, and that was dancing. No one from the mountains danced. But they watched. It was amusing to watch.

"Much too hard to speak a foreign language," she repeats after a moment, and I understand that I can go now.

It is dark when I come out, clear, still a black frost. A little dull to go back to the cramped room. But where should I go otherwise? To the café where the young boys hang over their one-armed bandits, grin and ask whether I haven't found myself any menfolk yet?

No thanks. Have fairly fresh rolls in the cupboard. And a beer.

Safely home I close the curtains, and lock the door to keep the most ardent tomcats away.

Hardly any writing is produced from this. A stupid idea. I should have gotten out of here a long time ago. She was not gracious, the young girl who was home at Christmas: "Sure enough, another one who is going to profit from Sami culture!"

The icy laughter.

I ought to get out of here.

It is God's will she is struggling with. Why He wants this and that. What He wants in keeping her here?

But there is more. There is the minister, what he was trying to say by dragging it out so long. Years have passed, but she hasn't gotten around to asking. Why did he let it happen? Why did he let the darkness fall over an open grave?

There is little I can help her with. I read a little when I am there. Would have sung if I had had a decent voice. I read. And it is while I read that I most strongly perceive that it is the wrong language.

All the same she thanks me.

He was exceptional. He did all sorts of work. Did women's work too. As soon as the umbilical cord was cut and tied he took over, thanked his sister-in-law with a young female reindeer and a cask of whitefish and sent her home to her family. She was back right after, but it was completely unnecessary, he took care of what had to be taken care of. People shook their heads at that, some laughed. "Men can be of many types," said the sister-in-law. She didn't laugh.

They knew that it would be a girl. Already before it began to show on her, they knew. She had gotten a sign. She had dreamt. She had dreamt that she was on a seasonal move. It was in the autumn, with packs. She and her mother, just the two of them, it was cold and wet, and they were freezing. But her mother was there, quite clearly.

When he came from the herd a couple of days later, she told him, that her traveling companion had been a woman. He smiled then. Said it would be nice for her to have company, someone to sew with, someone to keep house later on. Said nothing about him needing a hand. It certainly didn't occur to him. She always came first.

He built the finest sleigh seen in those parts. With a high back, broad and with plenty of room, tarred and shiny. New sheepskin furs he had taken care of the summer before, right after she told about the dream. Two soft, snow white furs. They weren't going to freeze during the migration, his girls. And they didn't either. Every time they stopped, he went back and tucked them in with gentle hands. She had tidied the child up, given her food, prepared the Sami cradle between her knees, put the furs tightly and warmly around them both. But he checked on them. Had to put his hand in before he took his place in front of the herd.

Behind her drove her oldest niece. She was clever, kept a long string of reindeer and everything they needed under control. She had her eye on one of the herders, she wasn't slow to ask, and her own folks had more than enough help.

Seldom had the spring migration gone so easily. It was as if fated for them, with an icy, sharp crust at night and just the right amount of melting while the sun was up. The reindeer got enough food. Everyone got enough rest. And better snow conditions they couldn't have dreamt about.

On the west side of the big mountain pass they released the female herd. The men herded the bull reindeer while she, her parents-in-law and niece took it easy at the calving grounds and had fine days. They took care of the females by turns. Everything went peacefully. There were fewer wolves now. Not like when she was a young girl. Then you could never be safe. It was worst when day was breaking. If the wolf hadn't managed to get the better of a single reindeer in the course of the night, it happened that it would rush through the herd in the tiny bit of light at daybreak and leave behind a smell so pungent that it frightened the reindeer in all directions. In that way it got its claws into one or another animal, and killed as many as it could reach.

Better days had come, in many ways. But you couldn't know how long it would last.

The year their daughter was born was a memorable year. The weather remained calm and not a single calf was lost.

They had arrived at the coast in the early morning one day at the end of May. The sea gulls wished them welcome. Those were strange sounds in the ears of the newly baptized girl. She was awake and good-natured, struggled to get her arms free.

Her mother folded the furs back, loosened the cradle straps and lifted the child high in the air while the little angel chortled and laughed.

"Have you ever felt God's presence in your heart?"

I shake my head.

"It'll come to you too. Good comes to the one who does good …
That's the way it is. You can't change that."

She grew up both strong and beautiful. Many continued to call her
the angel. Even when she became a big girl. The godparents were
proud of her. Everyone was proud. She was that kind who shone
with much light.

The weeks she spent at school in the village were a dark period for
her mother. At a loss she would sit on the wood chest during the
first days. Feed the stove, other work was difficult. It was he who
had to watch the pots, cook for them, cook for the dogs, look after
the ptarmigan snares, take care of the old folks, split wood and
carry it in.

Gradually it eased. She took up card weaving. Got colors into
everything that was black.

The minister was pleased with her. He told them. Said it the day
she was confirmed. Exhorted them to continue, with thanks and
admonitions and prayers, to care for one of the most beautiful
plants in God's acre.

And they promised.

She honored her mother and father. Was never afraid of work.

She had tamed her own draft reindeer herself. Tamed it the way it should be tamed. He was along, her father, was with her and saw to it that it went correctly. But only occasionally did he have to come forward and take the reins. Otherwise she struggled with it herself. She had a good approach, was agile and quick when she crept up on the side of the animal, from behind, at an angle, got hold of the rein, drew the rein, held it. He watched while she lay the hames over the neck, drew them under the chest, got the back straps guided evenly and nicely backwards and the straps from the loop under the chest she worked along the belly and attached them to the front of the sleigh, all this while she held on to the driving rein, taut, so there would be no doubt as to who was calling the shots.

The first driving tours ended with the sleigh overturned and her in tow with snow spray over her head, in her eyes, down her neck. Fully packed with snow and with laughter bubbling in her throat she was tossed hither and yon and in circles over the marshy open country while her father stood with the lasso ready to throw and reel them in when things got too wild. He chided the girl, what kind of crazy driving was she doing, and the girl laughed back that she was doing just as she had been taught to do, and what sort of teacher was he for that matter when things didn't go better!

She dug snow out of her neckband and the edges of her boot legs, unharnessed and tied the reindeer to a new birch tree. Then they emptied the sacks of moss, put the tips in the ski bindings and skied home.

Two such periods every day for three entire weeks – and she had the strongest and most willing draft reindeer of them all. It was a spotted three-year-old with powerful antlers. A magnificent animal to go to market with. And to the market she would go this spring, she was determined to do that. Now she was through staying home and taking care of the heat and cooking blood soup for the yelping dogs while all the other young people were in their best clothes, were in each other's company and having fun. She had sewed all winter. She had twelve pairs of moccasins and two pair of sealskin boots for sale to whoever wanted to pay. They could say whatever they wanted, her parents, but this spring she too was going to go.

Her mother had gotten a shock one day when the fox came right up to the door. It was a couple days before they were supposed to leave. She told this to her husband, but he just smiled.

Later, long afterwards, he told her about the fish. In a trembling voice he said that just before the trip to the market he had caught a strange fish in the lake with the many bays. He had fished there for years, but never experienced the like.

"She wanted so much to go," says the old woman. "It was impossible to hold her back. It was impossible."

The rest is fragments from many quarters. Her niece has no desire to talk either.

"It was destined," she says. "Everything is destined. Man doesn't rule."

They had traveled for over a day. The snow conditions were good, there was little snow that winter. The young folks had raced a bit along the river, and the girl who was on a market journey for the first time, was far ahead.

In the valley hollow on the east side of the green mountain they had settled down for the night, several families together, four tents in all.

They had eaten well and slept well and only had to pack up, load the food, canvas and poles in the sleighs and move on. It was the last stretch before the innermost part of the fjord. The young people had gone after the draft reindeer. They had been standing tied to the birch trees in a little grove nearby. The tent camp was right on the north side. There the sleighs stood ready, fully loaded with meat and hides.

It had resisted as soon as she came and was about to loosen the knot she had tied to the birch trunk the evening before. She hadn't seen such gestures in it before, she flinched, but was quick, tightened the rein, got hold of it, because she was so strong.

It was when she bent down to guide the rein under the belly and attach it to the front of the sleigh that it happened. She had turned, was almost ready, one little loop more – then everything was in place. If it had only been a little sooner. If she hadn't continued to turn, then it would have struck her shoulder or forehead. The forehead can take more. But now it hit so wrong, struck with its feet, several times, and hit where a person can least take it.

They say her mother was completely calm. She was the one who found out that the girl was still alive. They lifted her together, just the two of them, waved the others away, laid her in the best sleigh.

She nodded to him when he left. Stood still and watched him until he was out of sight. Then she took care of his string of reindeer, linked it up to her own. No one said a word. It was completely quiet in the camp group when they broke up and followed after.

She knew where she was going to find him. Knew well about the doctor's place, although she had never been there.

It was still light, and she recognized the draft reindeer from far off. It stood tied to the white fence.

The doctor's wife met her. A nice person, put her arm around her shoulder.

They had cut into the reindeer jacket and gotten it off. The same with her Sami jacket. She lay only in a thin linen shift in the white bed.

There wasn't much he could do, said the doctor. They just had to wait. They could stay there, and wait.

It has something to do with *that* night. Those days she squirms, sweats. The days she is silent, would rather that I just read. I know little about her nights.

The next time I come, the minister has been there. She seems light-hearted. Good-natured.

"Sit down. Did you come alone?"

"Yes –?"

"I see. I expected that you would find yourself someone."

I laugh. "Oh no, I don't think so. I've probably gotten too old."

"Old! Far from it, young as a blade of grass."

"I don't think I'll find anyone," I jest.

"Flying birds find."

We banter some more. It goes fine. Everything is far away. She asks me to push the button, she wants juice, I can have coffee, you just have to ask.

It is on such days that she takes me along, out and up into the mountains. After some brief introductory remarks about here and now. She never lingers, finds little to linger on. Then we are there. Outside.

"You should have seen it," she says. "You should have seen it when I came with my herd. His family didn't believe what they saw.

Everyone was outside, my sister too, she was already married into the same family. She knew, has, you know, always known that father earmarked mostly for me, and that that was just fit and proper. But the others, they didn't know."

She doesn't go further with this. I have it from her niece that a larger herd than hers no girl, neither before nor after, has brought into a marriage. But then she had worked hard for it too.

"You should have seen it in the fall," she says. "You should have seen when we slaughtered. The fat strip over the back was as wide as a hand. It was good food. It is bad to complain, but it is much poorer food you get now."

"You should have seen when we moved. When the herd flowed over the open country. It is as if the whole landscape sways, as far as the eye reaches. A finer view doesn't exist.
I don't know whether they see it any longer. They travel so quickly, with the machines."

This is one of the good days.
She doesn't ask what He wants in keeping her here so long.

No one knows what he did that night.

She probably doesn't know either.

They had found the animal, badly mauled.

A worse slaughter hadn't been seen.

But then it wasn't a slaughter either. It was ill treatment. Wolves and bears do no worse.

No one had seen him leave the doctor's place. No one had seen him come back either, but when they drove to the market place at dawn, there were fresh tracks in the new snow. His reindeer lay breathing heavily and resting very close to the white fence.

The one time she has spoken about it, she only said that they waited. Waited all night. And when it dawned, it was over.

She can't have escaped the gossip. Neither about the fine draft reindeer – nor about the other thing. She can't have escaped the glances, they are still sent. Even I see them.

It was a night with stars. A fine night to die in. The moon was new.

"Teach me Lord your way! I want to wander in your truth. Give me an undivided heart to fear your name."

Sometimes I give a start when she calls on God. I am not used to it happening so suddenly.

Of course she has heard it. It has been whispered the whole time. That sort of thing isn't forgotten. Neither that he went wild and attacked the reindeer, nor the other thing. Had it been another. But it was him, the last person one could expect it from. He had, of course, had his youthful sins, he just as others. But they had been put behind, long since. When he first got the faith, he stuck to it. Was God-fearing in silence, cooked only meat from his own herd.

Not that they had found anything by the large rock. Neither liquor nor money. But there were tracks. Clear tracks.

"One track is like another, it could have been anyone," says the niece, "don't come to me with tales."

What the old one thinks, no one knows.
Those, who come to visit her, all get to hear the same thing:
"By grace we are redeemed, that is God's gift."

A couple of times she has asked me what I want here. Whether I've gone away from something or come to something.
"You can't row straight with just one oar," she can say.
I know that there is a great lack in me. Alone you are no one. Here more clearly than any other place I have been. I say it is my work. Then she smiles:
"I see."
She for her part has been blessed. She got a God-fearing husband and a beautiful, obedient child.
"But they are gone. Everyone is gone. It is worst … But God is merciful, God has mercy…"

It is more and more this she dwells on. The other thing disappears gradually – the flash in the eyes, the wide-awake banter, the landscapes, sharply remembered, in detail.

She can twinkle, but is abruptly thrown out into this other thing:

"… life eternal, we who were dead by our trespasses and sins …"

She doesn't always recognize me. I must explain. Then it dawns.

"So you are still here! Did you find what you came for?"

I see that she is making an effort. Wasting her strength on me. I go less often now.

"Did you find what you came for?"

More than once I have had this feeling: She sees. She sees the surface and everything that is below. She has a glance that doesn't waver. In the beginning it made me embarrassed. Now it is more wonder that I feel. She locks me with her glance. Takes me along. First it was the landscape. Great and open. Now this: Her white, innocent child.

With few words, and without gestures.

No, it is not that she is squandering her strength on me. It is cowardice that keeps me away.

Her niece says that she is becoming confused. I think it is rather that she is tidying up.

We both stay away. More and more.

I go one Sunday. Reluctantly.

But no one can have everything unchanged.

So I go.

They have dressed her up for the day. She has a little silver brooch at the neck. She smiles, smiles and hums, incoherent, small fragments, but I recognize it, it is the same one as so often, and one of the few that I too know. *Then take my hands then.*

She breaks the sound off abruptly when she becomes aware of me.

Before she used to smile with her eyes, a little greeting of welcome, while she went on. Now she begins to struggle. As if she lost something when the door opened.

I greet her. She doesn't see me. Seeks something in the folds of the blanket, twists her head back and forth, but doesn't see, doesn't find.

I greet her again. Take her hands. She becomes calmer at once. Looks at me. Or through. I am not certain as to where she fixes her glance, but she fixes it.

She thinks I am someone else, talks to me in a language I don't understand. I try to explain, but it doesn't reach her. That is, I don't reach her, but the language does. She changes languages. An impulse was enough, she switched.

"... living with Christ, we who were dead by our trespasses and sins ... living with Christ. Sing! Sing to me." This time I have to. No matter how little I know. It is impossible not to do. I try to hit the note where she left off, can hear that I miss, hear that it grates, that I get lost. But anyway:

Then take my hands
and lead me forth
until blessed I end
in heaven's home.
I cannot walk alone
not even a step
Where You lead me alone
I will follow along.

"That was good," she says. Her voice as mild as she can make it. As if she wants to console me.
"That was good," she repeats.

They have pulled the curtains almost shut. Only allowed a narrow crack of light. It is so glaringly sharp at this time of year.

"You are nice." She gives my hand a weak squeeze. "The one who does God's will will have eternal life."
She breathes. Her chest swells. She draws new strength.
"God is merciful, He ..."
I can notice that she is dry in the mouth, that she is struggling to form words, her mouth will not obey. I ask whether she wants something to drink, and she asks for water. I lift her head and give it to her.

"Thanks, nurse," she says.

She sinks back on the pillow. Sinks into herself.

I get up, open the curtains a little more, as if I know that I will need sunlight for what is coming.

In the hallway hectic activity is heard. Feet running back and forth. Clatter and squeaking from beds being moved. An echo from instructions that reverberates through the walls. Someone eases the door open, sticks a nose in. Everything in order, out.

I sit and observe her hands. The distinct circulation through the veins, blue and sharp. White, soft skin. You would have thought her hands would be coarser, as much hard work as they have performed. But they are fine, – narrow and small. Impossible to imagine them with axe, knife, scraping iron, in bark lye, over coarse hide. Impossible.

Another one comes in, sees that she is sleeping. That I am sitting. And haven't the sense to leave.

It begins with a weak whimper. I hardly register it. Then it increases.

"I am here," I say and press her hand. "I am here, just rest, you rest."

The first thing I don't grasp, mumbling that fades away in a weak whimper. Then it becomes clearer, the voice carries:

"… sevenfold … like iron and your earth like copper … chastise you sevenfold …"

The voice rises, she gasps for air, opens her eyes wide, her eyes ramble, she doesn't find a point to fix on.

"I am here," I repeat, "just rest, it's me."

She tightens her grip on my hand, is strong, the white hand a claw.

"You shouldn't think …" she whispers.

"Not think?"

"He was pious. A pious man he was."

"Yes," I answer. "Yes, he was a very pious man, I have heard that."

Is it the shadow of a smile that crosses her face?

"God is merciful."

Her grip on my hand slackens.

For a little while she rests in this. A moment. Then her grip tightens, her body tenses.

The first part I don't catch, it is probably in her language, she is alone with that, I am shut out and only now do I notice that I am wringing wet, the room is suffocatingly hot, almost without air. But I can't get up. She is holding on.

"... the Lord is named Zealous, a zealous God he is ... the Lord is named Zealous ..."

The rest fades away in sobbing.

I try to reach her. Speak. Hum the melody from a little while ago. Speak again:

"You rest, God is merciful."

Words I have never used before.

"YES," she shouts.

And maintains it, with her hands.

"Yes."

As a weak sigh now.

Then stronger: "Your sin is forgiven you in the name and blood of Jesus. Jesus' name JESUS' NAME JESUS' NAME ..."

I grope for and find the alarm button, press, and continue to press until they come.

While I put on my coat, they manage to calm her. I don't know how, my back is turned.

I turn in the door, before I go. The last thing I see is Moses on Mount Nebo. He is looking out.

She lies there, calm and pale. One hand carefully pats the blanket, as if there is something she is trying to smooth out.

The Yellow One

She's right. That's the worst part. With regard to initiative and all that. I turn aside. Refuse.

I was going to refute something. That's the way it was. That's why I bit off more than I could chew.

I never learn!

The driver turned in toward a mountain hostel and announced a ten-minute coffee break. Hesitating, I padded after the other passengers. The young one with the windbreaker. And the older one. Her mother? Finally a sleepy young man with a knapsack and a gaudy jacket with Kawasaki on it. In large letters right across the back.

There were only the three, in addition to me.

A picturesque little café. Objects from the local culture in tasteful groupings, pictures of quality on the walls – woodcuts and watercolors. Not anything randomly scraped together here. There was style over this food stop in the middle of the desolate plateau.

I fumbled with my wallet, paid for coffee and lefse and crept into the back of the place, found a little table to myself. The driver sat down with the others. They ate and slurped coffee, chatted and stopped talking when the announced ten minutes were up, at least that much. Then he got up, our pathfinder, straightened his cap, took good hold of the moneybag.

"Is she ready now, the young lady?"

Everyone looked toward me, and smiled.

I slunk after. Plodded at the very back, in the nicotine smoke of the Kawasaki boy. She should have seen me, my good colleague and friend. Seen the arrogant sociologist out in the field. Gotten her theories confirmed about my many lacks, of which the ability to make up one's mind, make decisions was the most serious. It was bad enough at work. But worse with everything else. Which I sat still and let pass.

Now the young lady was ready.

As ready as she could be.

She's busy. She is always busy.

"Have some coffee, I'll be done soon."

Feeling at home I get a cup from the cabinet, press the button down on the coffee thermos. Magnum type, must hold two liters. I take a sugar cube from the package on the table.

The sewing machine purrs. She maneuvers cloth and ribbon under the needle, stretches one part, slackens another, guides them quickly, but straight, the edge of the costume pours forth. The needle goes like a sharp piston up and down, up and down, threatens to perforate her whole hand.

I look away, out into the air:

"You're working hard."

Slowly I pick up the finished front part, look at it, bold in its colors, sparkling, but stiff, hasn't been under the iron yet.

"Yeah, you have to. Can't sit around resting your head on your arms, that'll just bring you sorrows."

She is probably right. Some people have to be especially careful. Endure through work. Keep the head far away from the arms.

Busy constantly. That's the way it turned out. She is the last one who knows how. Her daughters have other things to do. Her daughter-in-law as well.

So she has to sew for them all.

Not so much to say about that matter. That's what has happened now, in so many homes. It was worse for their mother when only her younger son was still at home and got married to someone who locked the door. The old woman had expected to get someone to sew with when all her daughters had left her and gotten their own places. But the door in the new house was closed. Inside a shy creature was reading and was going to become something. He – the one who had bought her there – would have gone without shoes had his mother not been so good with her hands to the end. Much had faded for her, people and memories. But she sewed. It was in her hands, and didn't go away.

But she was sad. So many children, and then she was left sewing alone!

This is the past. If not so distant. Her mother had died in silence. A couple years ago now. Brusque and gruff she had often been, and for good reason, but fell asleep so sweetly. Not like her sister. The one who became childless early on and didn't glimpse peace in death, but arrived there with a shriek.

It is she who has told me that, she who is now sewing. It went on for rather a long time. It wasn't over until three days after I had last been there.

"It was nice of you to visit my aunt so often," she said on the day of the funeral.

"No problem," I said.

"Anyway," she said.

Now she sews. Her back bent, her shoulders tensed up, furrows between her eyes deep as a crater.

Until she suddenly knocks off, gets up, stretches her back with a long, loud yawn.

"That's surely enough for today," I suggest.

She rubs her eyes and groans. Hobbles to the kitchen counter, stiff and sore. Takes out a teacake from the icebox, lifts the big knife, cuts it up. She puts the cake plate in front of me, looks for some tobacco for herself. Sinks down in a chair.

"Good grief, what a grind. One person, and supposed to dress up the whole flock!"

One knife, one life, they used to say. When each and everyone looked after themselves. Now you have to look after many. It's exhausting. I see how exhausting it is on her entire, collapsed body.

She asks me to come again soon. They are not given to empty phrases, so she must mean it in a way. Find some sort of company in me, in spite of everything. I haven't much to offer. No matter what?

She knows about the newspaper. That I'm on leave. That I am working on a book. I didn't say that I was writing, that it had come to a standstill. She asks politely how it is going, and I say:

"Well, it's coming along."

It happened that she did the washing where I live – at the Mountain Hostel. Then we got to talking. I had just arrived. Beady in the eyes, completely green. Had I ever tasted marrow bones and broth? Well no, I hadn't exactly done that. Yes, then I had to come for a visit, she had just cooked, I could come along when she was done with the washing.

So quick. So easy. And already the second time I felt at home.

Or? I can sit for a long time and feel that way, be full, there's always food there – and warmth. Then something is said, I say something, or someone something, it becomes quiet, and she smiles, as if to a child.

It's a code I can't crack.

When I understood that I put my laptop away.

She was fortunate to get the washing job. There were many competing. In the beginning some looked askance at her. She understands them. Had someone else gotten it, she probably wouldn't have been any better either.

Now she has been washing for almost twenty years. It's hard, but steady, she knows what she gets, money in her account every month.

It didn't work the old way any longer. Not after all the new. It came so fast. Suddenly they hardly had enough for margarine for their bread.

It was a disaster, a disaster for many that the new times came like a landslide. But they have managed. For the most part.

"Yeah, there was a time … oh well."

I've understood that it was a long time. And that perhaps it isn't over. But this woman doesn't cry over spilt milk, abandon herself to the snow that fell, the streams that ran. She looks forward. Straight ahead. And doesn't waver.

It's the old story. She got pregnant. The girls fell for him, the hired hand at her aunt and uncle's. Had one here, another there. Two had children, she was one of them.

When the child, an unusually big and powerful child, was a half-year-old, he came on a courting trip with all that was required of a suitor. Not that that much was necessary. She was weak, without determination, like butter in his hands.

"It was destined."

That is what they say.

This strange saying.

Once she said it differently:

"I was a newborn calf. In an eagle's talons."

She laughed then. But the words were hard. As if hewn out of rock.

From her hands come the most beautiful things. In cloth – and leather. She is known for that. Many ask, come and plead. But she has her own to sew for, and there are so awfully many. Not that she has too many, I shouldn't by all means misunderstand her, I must understand her correctly, for God's sake.

Maybe it is the eagle's talons she feels she must pull back. He was always clever, she says. Began as a hired hand. But didn't take it easy. It was a nice herd they had in the end. And fat animals. Among the fattest.

He was a handsome man, I can see that? Still handsome. Even without teeth, he can laugh with an open mouth.

Anyhow, she has spoken about his courting trip on two occasions. Maybe three. He had fine gifts. There was nothing to complain about the gifts. Of course the silver brooch could have been larger, but the shawls were numerous, and rare, he never said where he had gone for them. She dressed up in those shawls for many years. Everyone said they were unusually fine. Even her mother said that when he opened the chest. She who otherwise didn't say so much. She was simply ecstatic, her grim face cracked.

"Unusually fine," she said.

When he left that time, it was with the same wry smile that had bowled her over.

She sat by the window in their little log cabin, with the shiny shawls in her lap. She laughed when she saw the string of reindeer start off and storm down along the river, past the house where the other girl lived.

"When he is tipsy, he walks around with his false teeth in his knit cap. That is fine, then he won't vomit a lot of money out into the snow."

She is not ironic. Quite soberly she just declares that he takes this precaution, her husband. And that it is a good rule.

It was hard on his stomach to be without teeth, she tells. The food didn't get chewed, lay there and burned.

There is concern in the way she speaks. Through the toughness, which she hews out of rock.

He had stumbled on his way from the Pub one evening. Had had a few beers too many. That was last year, during the hardest winter, pitch-black. If his friend hadn't also taken the shortcut through the loose snow, he would have remained lying there.

It comes entirely without expression. Impossible to interpret.

"If you want, I can teach you to sew."

She sits with a purse between her hands, of soft, tanned leather. For the Home Crafts Store, she says. She really doesn't have any time at all. Has two costumes waiting. But this is so pleasant a job. Pleasant as everything you don't have to do, I think. I've put the PC in the closet myself. To avoid looking at it. To avoid thinking about the advance I've used up.

How many purses would I have to sew to pay it back?

"Yes, I say, enthusiastic, – that could be fun."

She has done the trimming. Sits and irons the smooth leather pieces when he comes in. Caresses the smooth surface. Was that the way she sat when he drove home along the river, past the other house, with his whole escort?

Was it the fingertips' touch?

Was that what was necessary?

He glides over the floor, without a sound. Dress moccasins and the pleats in his Sami garb. If it hadn't been for the look, – the much too concentrated look. His mouth is narrow. Knit cap on.

He shuts the door to his own room, and locks it.

"Look, she says, – now you are going to see."

She lays piece against piece. Has threaded the needle. Sews the first stitches and hands the work smiling over to me.

The light lasts a long time now. It seems strange to have the curtains drawn. So I pull them back.

Sit and feel undressed.

The book about Africa I wrote in five weeks. I escaped both Christmas and New Years with it.

In Africa I lived in a big family. Everything I did was in broad daylight.

All the same I never felt undressed.

I could push it aside.

I wasn't English, French –

I came from far off. I put on the costume. And danced.

From here there are two roads to take.

One goes through the village. The other goes out of the village.

I get dressed and choose the latter.

When I come back, it will be dark enough to draw the curtains.

I walk fast. As if I have a goal. Here you don't walk just to walk. She never walks.

I asked whether she skied. That was on the first visit.

"No," she laughed, "not any more. But before – when we set the ptarmigan snares and fished in the lakes and in the river. In the old days we used to ski constantly."

I'll have to see about Easter. When the other tourists come.

I keep well to the side of the road. Flinch every time a snowmobile comes. They have no business being on the road. They're there anyway. Have only mediocre steering on the hard surface. Last Christmas a young girl was mowed down. She was fortunate to escape. Broke a leg.

I jump out into the snow bank every time.
Let them just grin.

It was right after New Years, I think. I don't know where everyone was. Whether there was something special on TV. Or was it Bingo. Radio bingo perhaps – on the local station.

In any case – I walked the same route: From the Mountain Hostel, past the gas station where two abandoned pumps stood shining, over the bridge, further on where the houses are more spread out, one or another little cluster along the shore, apartment houses with yellow light in the windows, the contours of a blacked-out cow barn, a shed –

Then, in the course of a short hour, a half hour maybe, I understood how it once had been: Hint of sound, tiny vibrations, murmur from the frosted dwarf birches that cowered together like shivering elves, a delicate, fine murmur. And further away – the river ice with a playing of sounds, high, low, a weak roar, dark, and one long, bright note, persistent, above the others, unbroken, while the rest of the instruments entered, died away, and entered again. But the whole time – one long, white note.

I had come to a standstill, for the creaking steps pierced my ears.

I stood. I don't know how long.

Only when I was back at the Mountain Hostel did I feel how frozen stiff I was.

I supposed that probably there is a language in the ice.

Maybe that's what she meant, the old one, she said: "The young don't know when you can walk on the ice. They don't have time to listen."

I have fairly decent technique on the purses. Have almost taken over the entire production already. She had to get back to the sewing machine. They'll be coming soon. One from the south and one from the west. One has work. But her mother can't see that any money comes from it. The other has an exam. Always one exam or another.

"Yeah," she sighs, "it's hard to get ahead today, you have to have schooling."

She doesn't have more to say about this. She is not talkative as far as the children are concerned. Gets to the point quickly.

"The one who talks a lot, has a lot to answer for," she said once. She wasn't referring to the children then. Nor him. It was the neighbor. The one who is so industrious in paying visits. He has stories.

"Don't tell him anything. He twists it his way. A bad person is worse than a juniper fire."

So I do as she has taught me. I answer in monosyllables. Keep my eyes on my sewing. She on hers. Until he gets tired and leaves.

"He has a smart wife," she tells me afterwards, "she shuts her ears."

She herself prefers to speak about times past. Those were good times. People helped each other. They had always done that. The present time is a wolf's time.

She remembers the war. It probably sounds strange, she says, but she has such good memories.

It was late fall when they fled up into the mountains. Some had torn down their houses, spread the materials around so that there would be something to build up from afterwards. They lived cramped in the tents during the period they were in hiding. And cramped afterwards, in the few houses still left. But never did they feel they were in anyone's way. They packed as many as possible in the small log houses. During the night they lay so close that they bumped into each other at the slightest movement. They dug into the ashes, rebuilt, worked hard all day long. They got turf they had stored in outlying fields, put up turf huts. It must have been dark, and cold. But you remember only warm bodies – and laughter.

"Nowadays it's different. You give something to the dog and get rubbish in return.

Yes, they worked all right," she says. "Carried water, carried wood, the house full of children, her own and others, – and old folks, bedridden. All needing care. You had to hang in there.

But when they sat down, they were at peace.

There is another sort of weariness now. It goes right into the bone. And is there the whole time."

She doesn't know when it began. Of course, everything has gotten easier, in so many ways.

She remembers when they hooked up the electricity. She had thought the light would be white. Like that of the Coleman lanterns. But it was yellow. She can still picture the yellow faces around the table. They're drinking the first coffee she has made on the stove.

The stove is a good thing.

But then came the rest. And it was a lot.

He slaughtered constantly, it had gotten easy to sell; the road was open all year.

It had gotten easy to buy too. Anything imaginable.

Just one thing got harder. Visiting relatives on the other side of the mountain. It was a long way to drive around. When the winter road came, the snowmobile bus stopped going.

They talked about everything new. What they had and didn't have. The sort of thing they had never talked about before.

On the headland they had had a television set for several months before the broadcasts reached here. It got crowded on the headland when it started up. Everyone came and looked. She went too, and she said to her husband that it might be interesting to have such a device. Not that she had so many hours. On the contrary, her hands constantly full.

But when the others bought –

"Now everyone sits, separately, and stares. And those who still go anywhere, don't always have good intentions."

I get to take along a purse. Must have one myself of course, she says.

So I'll remember. For I might be leaving soon? There's nothing much for me here?

She looks at the ceiling.

"Your children are grown," I say, carefully.

She shakes her head. Smiles.

And in that smile lies everything I am unable to reach.

The newspaper writes about the readjustment program. Just window dressing, a few say, – death by starvation. A necessary step to stimulate departure from the livelihood and thereby prevent ecological catastrophe, others say. Reindeer and people must be reduced otherwise a wasteland will be next.

The neighbor liquidated first. Her husband right after. Got cash money in his fist. Promise of more money in five years.

But after that?

The one walks around to the houses.

The other one walks around with his knit cap pulled well down over his ears.

"You shouldn't complain," she says, "but it is bad now when you don't have as much as a hide to scrape."

She laughs. A short, hollow laughter.

"Yeah. It is worse for the young people," she adds, "when they quit, without anything. While we old folks … no, it's all the same."

She usually says: *The old folks.* In a way she is right. She has lived a long time. Through several epochs.

"That's when you should have been here. Before. It was fun. We were so many. When we moved, we were four families in the group. Four tents. That can sound laborious today, but we got right to it, didn't waste any time in getting the tents either up or down. The oldest young people helped cut firewood and brush, strip birch bark. Of course we had some with us, for on the bare rock, out by the coast, there isn't much to find. Yeah, you should have been here then. We were comfortable in the tents. Cramped and comfortable.

You can believe that it is nice up there, when the weather is good. It happened that we rested during the night without putting up tents, just stopped and cooked meat, sat around the bonfire until it began to get light. Then we went on. Drove until the sun softened the crusty snow, then we stopped and slept.

No, it wasn't hard to move. Not when you are healthy and can work. I have good sisters-in-law. One of them had only one child, it was one she had from before, so she helped with mine. For the most part we had five reindeer strings. It was us, the womenfolk, who took care of them. The menfolk had the herd. And it wasn't small then. It was among the largest."

There is a click in the lock. He opens up and walks through the room. Out. Pulls four times on the starter cord without getting the motor started. On the fifth try it kicks in. Coarse-grained snow is kicked up out in front of the wall. The spray hits the windowpane, covers it.

Soon the roar of the motor is gone.

"It wasn't always like this," she says, calmly.

"No?"

She divides a sinew thread. Twists it against her cheek.

He is quick this time. Parks on the other side of the house when he comes back. Walks just as quietly through the room as before. Unlocks. Opens. And locks.

She doesn't look up. Looks at her sewing.
"Life isn't sugar," she says.

The first years were good. She had been fortunate. The other one was still unmarried.

He put up a house, then they had their own place. Then she was pregnant with number two. The one who works out west.

She was still like butter, and soon they had three.

They had four when they got electricity. Good heavens, everything was so easy. Warm in the house. Hot water in the tap.

It cost a little, of course. He had to slaughter more.

It cost everyone. But others were reluctant to slaughter their own.

So they had to be more careful.

It wasn't entirely easy. He did his best. But everyone needs to sleep, one time or another.

The older son wasn't of much help for long. He had a restlessness in him. The upshot was that he was going to try school.

And he tried.

And came home. Hadn't been happy. There were several who weren't happy, who also came home, so they couldn't find fault with him.

They tried to get him up to the mountains. But it was useless. He had an unwillingness. Didn't have it in him.

Then he tried the mine. That worked out for a while.

Then he tried school again. And came home.

Entertained himself by driving around on the snowmobile.

Yeah, he had to do something you know.

But it was expensive. The others had snowmobiles for several years without anything falling apart, they just changed the belts. But with them! Always something.

He traveled around aimlessly, he who had taken over the earmark from his grandfather, drove back and forth, along the river and along the road, drove the snowmobile into the ground.

There stood his father.

Couldn't go anywhere.

"People are not stones," she usually says. "We are no more than people."

He is supposed to be down south now. I have asked where, but not gotten any clear answer.

"Down south."

The other son was happy in school. Was simply too happy. They haven't seen either him or their daughter-in-law in two years. He is something technical, in an office. She is also something fine. They have a daughter four-years-old. Lisbeth is her name. Speaks only Norwegian.

"When the children are small, they trample on your lap. When they get bigger, they trample on your heart."

That's the way she put it, the old woman.

I checked out a load from the library. Picked rather randomly. Everything from *Lapp Mythology* to the *NOU Report* Number 18, 1984. *On the administration of justice for the Sami.*

But I am restless. I think it is the light. This all too intense light. I have taken two ski tours.

I am a tourist after all.

One evening I take a walk after the evening news. Have kept myself in the 'rented room' for a few days. You shouldn't overstay your welcome, I've learned. But then she knocked on the door one day when she was washing. Wondered whether I had abandoned them.

She sits and sews like mad. Her eyes are bloodshot. She is running out of time, she says. She has to go to the doctor with a swollen finger. You get rather helpless. No one nearby to utter charms for the least thing.

A half day passed. Now she is behind. The girls are coming this weekend.

I ask whether there is something I can help her with. She hems and haws.

I could perhaps learn to do the pleating?

She finds the iron and damp cloth. And a little cutting board. She shows me. Raises the board on edge. Every pleat must be pressed against, hard, until the steam from the wet cloth diminishes. Then it'll hold. Then you will have a pleat that will hold.

She herself sits on the opposite side of the table. Has one eye on the machine and one on the iron.

We take a break after a while.

"You're good," she says.

"Oh, I don't know, think it's a bit uneven."

"No, it's very nice."

I am not sure whether she is telling the truth. Maybe she must take what she can get. There is no more time. Everyone has to sleep, some time or other.

I suggested one day that for some there is perhaps too much time. But she shook her head.

"Everything is better than war."

I happen to think about the old woman. She told me something once. It was a sort of tale. A myth perhaps.

It went like this:

Before the end of the world the tongue will turn black and the raven white. The reindeer will make new antlers in the winter, be scraped completely bare at the top of the head and become so wild the people can't handle them. And there will be such discord among people that everyone will be afraid of each other. And hunger and high prices, plague and death. All the menfolk will be drafted for war and die there. Only their clothes will be left that the women can kiss. Finally they'll kiss the tracks where they have walked, and cry.

She gets up and lights the ceiling lamp.

Now I notice it too. That the light is yellow.

The present, as she calls it, is yellow.

The neighbor comes over to see whether any of the daughters had a swelling in the stomach. He inspected them, without embarrassment. Asked whether they came alone, whether they brought anyone along.

He got guffaws in reply. Then he left.

The meat kettle stood brimming on the stove, and the girls helped themselves.

"Eat," she said to me too. "Eat now so you don't completely disappear." She had asked me to come. I had thought about staying away this day, but she insisted. I didn't really feel like it, I had met her youngest child at Christmas.

They studied the Sami outfits. The smell so fresh that it nearly flew off them.

The border a little too narrow, the one thought.

A little too dark a material. That was the other one.

Their mother shrugged her shoulders.

They went to bed. Had traveled far. Especially the youngest one. Three hours' flight from the south.

He came in a half hour later. Headed straight for the kettle. We heard him help himself. Heard the chair scrape against the floor when he sat down. Now and then a sharp sound of the knife against the edge of the plate. Otherwise it was quiet.

She had mentioned the silence once. I think I had just arrived. She told me what they were engaged in, what they had been engaged in, to put it more correctly. And that he had stopped. Sold. Sold the whole herd.

"It has gotten so quiet," she said. "Everywhere. When you no longer have anything to talk about. You meet people. You know them. And then it's as if you had never seen them before.

Everything is gone. Just silence left."

She was still sitting in the easy chair when I left. As if sunk down into a mold. The cigarette pack had fallen onto the floor. Her eyelids blinked.

Outside it was blowing. The new layer of snow was swirling up, bored into your nose, blocked out your vision.

I walked with one hand over my forehead. My fingers got stiff in the wool mittens.

She belonged to a dexterous lineage. That she had told me once. Said it wasn't everyone who had a sense for color. Some are too fond of yellow, others green. And too much white just seems foolish. I have seen it. There are only a few who manage to create harmony out of a jumble of colors and ribbons. She can.

Now she is resting. Sunk into her mold. Fills the chair. For a while.

I throw myself down on the bed. My face and fingertips are burning after the sharp, biting wind. I lie there on fire, remember things she has said:

He had been a playful father. Took them along often. He took them to the timber forest in the fall when the trees he had felled in the early summer were well dried and ready for trimming. He let them use the axe early on. They were good at it. The oldest too, when he had time, when he got up from the mound he was sitting on or came down from the tree he was hanging in and took a turn.

They all got strong. By twos they lifted the fattest logs from the hill, carried them away and raised them up to the sky. There they stood, with pale trunks and of fine quality, waiting for winter snow conditions, waiting for them to return, take the wood home on the sleigh.

He taught them to flay the leg hide and to throw a lasso. Stuck antler crowns in the hill and showed them how you threw firmly.

And they threw in competition, had a good time.

He took them along to the cloudberry bogs. For hours they walked in mosquito swarms thick as porridge. Kept going with the thought of food and coffee, hung in there. He joked with them during the breaks, had stories. They waved the mosquitoes away and laughed.

She can talk like this. About the children when they were still children.

The lasso throwers have gone to bed. With white city hands they each went over their costumes critically. And went to bed.

And he who could laugh with an open mouth –

Now he shuffles over the floors, a dog that sniffs his way over to the kettles. Goes back, to where he came from. A closed room.

And silence.

There is one daughter I haven't seen. Haven't heard much about either.

"She is married," her mother says tersely.

At the Mountain Hostel I've heard that she is supposed to be as shy as an owl. The female manager has told how she looks too.

So it is probably for that reason she comes so seldom.

"Not much to come to." Says her mother.

He spoke with me once. Came out from the closed room, and spoke.

I mostly noticed his hair. So thick and black. The wry smile she had spoken about I couldn't detect, but he was politely interested. A quiet man with the usual questions. Where from? How long? Many siblings?

Then he left. Stroked his hand through his hair when he left.

As if he could feel my eyes.

Or was it that his head got too bare, without cap.

They are invited to a wedding. That's why the new costumes were a rush job.

Two whole days, seven hundred guests. Two large families had strengthened their ties to each other one more time. It was worth celebrating.

"Ugh, these two day weddings. I don't understand how they manage. Drunks and snotty brats and gossip, it is so repulsive!"

The tired seamstress seems reluctant. She would probably have preferred to stay at home – both the first, pretty day and the second.

But has to get away, she too. Dress up the girls, dress up herself, fasten the silver brooches to their chests, be visible.

She can no longer count on him.

So she has to be visible for both of them.

The girls go willingly. Thank God. Go cheerfully the two days. If they behave decently, they can show off their mother – her skill, the straight seams, the colors that don't clash, but float through the room like northern lights, the fluttering lower hem, the bobbing motion over thirty yards square.

Now I understand that it wasn't only for their sake that she sewed. Sewed until cramps and sleep overtook her, alternately.

I see the new zeal in her hands when she dresses them. See the trembling fingers when she puts the silk shawls over their shoulders. She arranges with one hand and holds the other firmly on the corner at the back. It must not be lopsided, must by all means not be lopsided, otherwise they will become widows.

"So what?" says the one, with a laughter that raises a racket in the room of trembling hands and quiet expectation about everything that will soon be displayed.

It is the one with the all the exams who laughs.

A faint blush sweeps over her mother's face.

"Besides we have to get married first," she continues to laugh loudly, with a stiff neck and her mother's index finger concentrated against the smooth silk at the back.

Her mother cannot answer, she has four safety pins between her lips. It is not certain that she would have answered if her mouth were free either. She is of the discreet sort. Not with a single word has she ever mentioned what I lack. Her aunt was freer of ostentation, in her mild, jocular way.

She doesn't say in plain words what her daughters lack either. It isn't necessary. Everyone knows she had wished there were more than three silver brooches she was fastening to the one girl's bosom more fully ripened than the other.

"Yes, now it is Juvvin Inga's turn," she said that day I was pleating. "She's going to become the wife of John Mattis, son of Issat Ante himself, you can bet she is rather proud."

Then she continued to sew. I did the pleating. During a break she talked about her own suitor. I don't know how many times she'd done it, but now she painted the picture. I could hear the reindeer sleigh cut through the snow, the creaking in the frozen hinges when he opened the door. Could see the steam from the thawing group in the weakly lighted log cabin. And the shawls – so smooth that they tickled the palms of my hands.

Never had more tender meat been eaten and richer bullion drunk. Never had a finer suitor been better spoken for, and never had a marriageable guy gone out into the winter cold more satisfied than he after having left the box with the silver brooches and finery with her.

I got to hear about the wedding too.

Three couples went in front and an unending line behind, two by two, on a calm, sunny day all the way to the church door. Inside they sat packed in like sardines. Everyone had come. The family of the other girl too. Didn't want to appear rejected.

She puts her hand on her face. Only her eyes show. Narrow, clever crevices.

She is full of memories.

They cheer her up.

The third daughter comes too. Husband and car. The largest silver brooch covers her whole bosom. Rattling armor. She herself is of the silent type. She and the youngest one, the one who comes from the south, alike as berries. And at the same time so unalike that you wouldn't believe they sucked from the same breast, followed in each other's footsteps.

Her mother greets her smiling. Greets her husband too. Not so fully smiling, I note.

Her husband sits down, finds a magazine to flip through.

Mother and daughter turn as if on an invisible signal and go out into the hallway.

They come back separately. The daughter first. She had a yellow shawl on when she arrived. Now it is pink.

Both sisters look up, but don't exchange glances. This is the sort of thing that happens tacitly.

She had wanted to dress me up too, and take me along. The more, the merrier, I gathered. Yet I couldn't manage it. But I'll go along to the church to take pictures.

The pink silk shawl is pretty on the pale skin. Her eyes roam, but meet mine a couple times, friendly.

Her father has come out of his room, but is not dressed for the wedding. Shakes hands with his son-in-law first, without gestures and without words. The young man briefly lifts his eyes and hands from the magazine.

He goes on to his daughter, calmly. A quick, light handshake. But something drifted over his face, a short second. It could resemble a smile, it could almost resemble what she has tried to tell me – about the playful, the wry.

It's time to gather everyone into the fold.

She looks confident, the mistress of the house, as she strides out into the sunlight. Handbag with hymnbook over her arm. Her daughters behind, taking small steps, afraid of slipping in their finery.

She sits down in the back seat with the married couple. I sit in the back of the second car.

The girls leap into the front seat from opposite sides. The youngest one drives.

They are quiet on the trip. What are they thinking about?

Have they also heard about the suitor with the straight back – rushing down along the river ice?

Do they also wonder what had bent that back?

Or perhaps they know.

In the same way that they know about their sister. That she has black and blue spots under her clothes like a map of Finland.

And that there is nothing they can do.

They sit quietly in the front seat.

Their laps full of splendid ribbons.

"It was during his time of strength. He could keep watch. Came home with meat, rested, helped with the woodcutting and left again. The children were small. We probably lacked a lot, if you think back. But we didn't think about it. Everyone lacked the same things. On Sundays it happened that we packed the children into the sleigh and visited my sister who is married to the farmer on the other side of the river. They had three cows at that time. Clabbered whole milk with sugar and crumbs was the best thing the children knew of.

He never had time to be at home for long.

The youngest one used to cry when he left again.

There was still peace for the most part. The herd grazed. He found it where he left it, provided it was a good year without bare spots.

But it changed.

I don't know exactly when."

And he?

She reads from my face and adds:

"Everything changed."

It's an ordinary day and the girls have left.

The one who came with her husband, stayed only one night, or not even that, it was hardly morning when they left again.

The youngest stayed longest. A good week.

"Once we lost twenty animals in one night. We found blood and buckshot. But no tracks. The wind had come up before the sheriff's people arrived. No tracks either from snowmobiles or sleighs.

He disappeared then. Gone for several days.

Hid himself like a wounded animal."

"Best to forget. That's the best.

Not everyone is suited to fight. You have to be a wolf yourself. Only the hardest are able. It's not worth it. When you only have yourself to fight for. No others. What good would it do?"

She gives a clear signal, no mistaking it. When she has said enough, she indicates it by getting up, grasping for something, stopping.

You don't miss it.

Soon the washing machine is going in the bathroom.

It thaws. I trudge along the side of the road. In a week everything has turned into slush. Coal black snowdrifts. The snowmobiles get stuck in a wet sea and just spin. Cusswords and smoke climb from the open ground.

This day I've neither seen nor heard him.

Yet I am certain he was there.

I circle around myself. Walk. And turn.

Who can draw a clear line between curiosity and something else?

I lie down on the bed and search for the clear line.

Melting snow everywhere. Provided you don't get yourself up into the hills – to dry snow and ptarmigan cackling.

But it's a ways there.

I have tightened the loops around my skis. They stand in one corner.

It is not many the words she has said about what she calls the war. Just that the cost is broken bonds. Neighbors who look straight ahead. The old one talked about this too. Said that's what happened when people no longer read in the book after they have been confirmed.

"But ..." she added, "they weren't unacquainted with it before either. It was worst in the autumn when the furs were thickest, darkest and softest.

There were those who came to church in newly sewn, shiny reindeer jackets, entirely without shame."

"Oh, you lamb of God," she whispered softly, so that it could scarcely be made out.

"Oh, you lamb of God who bears the world's sin."

I saw her tears then.

"It's gotten so crowded, that's how it is. You have to be big to hold your position. It's a hard struggle. You have to have expensive hands. Or sons."

That's the way her niece explains it.

I've never seen tears in her eyes.

Maybe she doesn't have any.

I met a fox with a nearly hairless tail one day. Told it to her.

"It'll be the end of the world when the dogs attack each other and the fox has no fur," she said.

She is of the sort that never raises her voice.

Everything is said with the same calm.

I brought up her oldest son again, right after Easter.

Since I was going to leave soon, I said.

And since it was down south he was.

Perhaps nearby?

Just then some of her calm slipped away.

She shook her head. "No," she said. "No, it's not worth it."

Her voice broke, but she pulled herself together again.

"He doesn't want to."

Firmly now.

"We have tried. His sister who lives there … He doesn't want to."

There was a pause. I don't know how long.

She hid her eyes from me, found a spot on her apron, wetted her thumb with the tip of her tongue and rubbed.

I had gone too far. And found no easy way out. I had forgotten that she is reluctant to speak about anything in the present.

She sat with a ring of sweat beads at her hairline and energetically rubbed an invisible spot.

Then she got up, wiped her hand over her forehead, opened the window.

It was so quiet that you could hear the seething of the snow melting next to the wall. Fresh fragrance penetrated into the room.

A snowmobile roar approached, came very close, and died away. A motor was shut off.

"It'll be spring soon."
She looked up, assumed a light tone, and smiled.

He came in with two plastic bags full.
Nodded to the guest, straight in the eye. I nodded back.
He had been shopping. She jumped up and put the things away.
They exchanged words. Mild, as far as I could tell.
Then he went out again. Greeted spring with a bare head.

She had a lightness in her movements when she came into the living room again.
It didn't take much.

Perhaps it is because I'm about to leave. Something to do with it not being as dangerous. I'll be taking it with me after all. Won't spread it around here.

Therefore it is good that she opens up.

Piecemeal and barely. But more than before.

It comes helter-skelter. So much that has been blocked. Now everything is going to come out at the same time. Mixed up. And she stops. Opens up again. And stops.

I see that it is an unfamiliar effort. That her whole body is struggling to pull it out:

She has never been one of those who fished with a silver hook.

They had had a hard time at home. Her father was of the sort that preferred to stick around the house. Her mother had to be everywhere at the same time.

…

She was along to the market that time her cousin died. Saw her – at the doctor's home. With her hands folded.

She remembers that she's thought about how it would have been if it had been she who was struck by the hoof. Whether her parents would have grieved for her the way she saw her aunt and uncle grieve.

She wasn't able to picture it.

…

She met him early.

He had been there as long as she could remember.

She was too young, but he waited for her.

As well as could be done.

She has no regrets, if I can believe that.

There hasn't been anything to regret.

"Everything is destined."

The thin cigarette she is puffing on has gone out. She lights it again.

One early spring while the children were still small she was sick in bed for more than a week. She had a high fever and wasn't able to get up. He got her youngest sister, she took over everything, took care of her, night and day, took care of the children and the house. He sat on the wood box. Wasn't able to get away. This was just before the spring migration. The female reindeer had begun to get uneasy. The herd had to be tended the whole time. The others in the *siida*[2] were there of course, on shift, but it wasn't enough, he hired a herder.

When she got better again, he was so happy. Took his son up on his knee, said that as heavy as he had become, they would soon have a hand themselves, didn't need to hire if something went wrong.

The boy had looked so serious. Not a hint of pride or a smile on his face.

One time he went through the ice, the older boy. It was a neighbor who pulled him out. He was there, it so happened, was on a trip into the mountains and had a lasso over his shoulder, heard a shout.

His father kept watch over him for two days.

He wasn't very sick. A little fever and cough.

But his father sat there. For two whole days.

For safety's sake.

---

2. Small group of families.

"He'll come. He'll surely come when it's time."

She ascertains. With a steady voice.

But her whole body stoops.

"He'll come, the other one too. When he's grown up. When he knows. I have sewed for the little girl. Moccasins, everything. I sent it. They can do what they want with it."

…

"We taught them everything.

It was a waste of time."

…

"The last dog we had for ten years. It liked to ride on the snow-mobile. Was quick to jump up on the seat when someone started. Clung to it.

It was a good dog. Made himself useful.

He was good company too. Very good company."

It's a jigsaw puzzle she is doing.

She wants to share it with me.

But I'm not good at that sort of thing. Have never been.

She has to do all the pieces alone.

"They didn't want this."

She lets her eye sweep over the room, out. Between the borders of the light curtains lies the sloping, wooded hillside above the river. Sparse brushwood down below. But bare toward the top. Snow and sky merge with each other. The dividing line is wiped out by mist.

"None of them. They want another life. No hair and no fur and no filth. He has to understand that!"

The last part comes with new force, she straightens herself up.

Before she sinks back again.

"He thinks it is his fault, the older one. That all the pressure was put on him."

Her glance is turned inward. I'm not sure whom she is talking to. "It's gotten so quiet," she sighs.

…

"We shouldn't have put the dog to death.
We should have kept it. Kept … something."

The rest is without words. I don't know what it is she screams, with her distorted face, entirely without sound. Only her shoulders that shake.

I'll have to wait a few hours at the airport; the bus leaves early. That's fine. Fine to take it little by little.

She said she could drive me, but I answered that it wasn't necessary. Nor did she insist. But she has asked me to come for a short visit. I must have meat and broth before I leave, she said, – so I have something to travel on.

Strange to take the last walk.

The sun has gone down, and it has begun to freeze. Thin crusts of ice lie on the puddles, break when I step on them.

The cars that drive by are covered with icy water, mud and clay. Toward evening it hardens. Their bodies are all equally gray.

I know that the herds are moving now, but you don't see it in the village. There is just as much traffic, the noise just as blaring, the snowmobiles just as many. At any rate, almost. Only the stray dogs are fewer.

I take off my snow boots on the steps, but carry them with me and set them right inside the door.

The smell of newly cooked broth hits me when I come into the hallway.

The air is full of steam.

It is unusually quiet this day. No clattering of containers, no sewing machine humming. The TV is on, but without sound. She sits facing the flickering screen and jumps when I come.

"Didn't you hear me?" I ask, embarrassed for having barged in so suddenly. I thought I had been careful to clear my throat in the hallway, as I usually do. Haven't been able to get used to just walking right in.

"Sit down," she smiles. "I think I fell asleep. Oops …

Come in. Sit down there."

She points toward the empty chair.

Only now do I see him. Curled up on the sofa. He has laid one arm over his head. His face is hidden. He lies at the very edge, his knife sheath dangles in open air.

Then I recognize the stench.

And it's not broth.

"It's … no problem? That he …"

She scrutinizes me.

"No. No, of course, by all means."

I don't find anything else to say. Wanted to have said something … easy, about it being nothing to bother with, a bagatelle –

She gets up.

"I have meat for you."

Eagerly she beckons me along out into the kitchen.

The large casserole is on the stove.

On the counter is a dish with marrowbones.

"You don't like them cold?"

She doesn't wait for an answer, moves them carefully back into the hot kettle.

Soon she has dished it out.

The table is loaded with all the best.

We let him rest.

We keep our eyes and talk to the food.

I can't remember the last time I ate so much. I try to stop her, but she keeps ladling it out. Splits the bones with one chop. The knife light as air in her hand, but it strikes with the force of a sledgehammer.

We finish with cloudberries and whipped cream. She had hidden them in the icebox. Takes the large glass bowl out as a surprise after I am stuffed.

Then the door moves.

Cold evening air filters in.

Soon he is standing in the doorway.

"Well?"

"Well?" he says one more time when he sees the man on the sofa.

She continues to eat, nods to me that I should do the same. It's him. The neighbor, the juniper fire.

We take small mouthfuls, let the whipped cream melt.

"Well, has he lost his knit cap?"

He guffaws. "Oh yeah, that was quick."

Guffaws even more.

We take new mouthfuls of golden cream. I have no room for more, but let the spoon go. She can't have much room either, but moves her arm slowly up, and down, fills the spoon, up, into her mouth, and down.

She looks at me. Smiles.

I smile back.

We charm him away with a smile.

Out in the hallway he tries one more dry laughter, but it gets stuck, turns into coughing.

"Good lord, that it is possible to get so full!"

She groans.

We groan in chorus, and laugh viciously at him walking stiffly away on the ice, we can see him under the curtain – shaking knees, his arms swinging in all directions.

I say something about her being clever, quick-witted. Something like that.

She answers calmly, almost humdrum:

"The one who lets herself be eaten by insults, withers."

We move back to the living room. She doesn't let his snoring bother her. Nor the sudden gasps he emits. As if in pain.

Her lips are curled a little, she nods toward his knife sheath.

"He hasn't gotten used to going without it.

That's the first thing he does when he gets up in the morning, she says, – puts his belt on. Is sort of not dressed without the knife."

He earmarked for them the whole time, she tells. For the girls too.

When they were home, he told them what kind of animals he had picked out for each one individually.

Since the calves weren't much to describe, he described the mother. The color of the pelt, the shape of the antlers. They listened with half an ear.

Eventually not even that.

They had their thoughts in entirely different places.

One of his legs hangs over the edge, is about to drag him along.

She sees it, reaches out, lifts his foot up, shoves it against his lower leg, pushes him further in on the sofa.

"There," she says, and gives him a slap on the knee.

The whole thing surely takes no more than a couple seconds. Yet, it is as if the scene is frozen. As if the image remains and shakes.

The foot that slides. Her arm, a plump arm in a flowered material, that calmly reaches out, a firm hand against his lower leg, a goal-directed motion, from the edge of the sofa and inward, into place. A tiny slap, so little that it would have been imperceptible had the scene not been stopped on the reel, frozen.

Now I saw it.

"We are brought up to work and get by," she says calmly.
That's what we are used to.
Nothing else.

I have nothing to say. Don't know whether there is anything to say to this.

I see that his foot wants to drift back. Inch by inch it slides along the large-patterned material.
I notice that I'm waiting.

Everything is different this day, it occurs to me. It isn't just that he is lying there. It is something else. More.
There are the same photographs on the walls – confirmation candidates, bridal couples, colorful pictures in golden frames.
The same sharp colors on the rugs and curtains.
Everything apparently as before.
And yet changed. Both the room and she –
Then I see it.
It is her hands. They lie in her lap. Uneasy they lie there, without anything to hold onto. Neither material nor leather. Nothing.

Now she too becomes aware of his foot.
His whole lower leg has drifted over the edge. Hangs heavy. Pulls.
She looks at me, inquisitively. Can I give her a hand?
I get up. She gets up too.
Carefully we lift him up, we each put an arm over our shoulders.
Then we take hold of his hands. Hold on.
He hangs as if lifeless between us.
Carefully we haul him in to his room.

And The Red One

I hadn't been so terribly self-confident the last time either. But it was easier then. Not just that I had less baggage to lug along. Sandals and cotton dresses somehow don't weigh so much. No, it wasn't that. I was in a way still drifting. Had my college days in my body. They were slipping by.

The packing for this trip I had been doing for weeks. Put in a wool sweater, changed my mind, put in a different one. Had been totally occupied and struggling with purses and bags until I was completely finished. In the end I didn't know what I had with me. Apart from the PC and the exclusive portfolio with sheets of paper and envelopes that Siri had brought along the last day on the job. She wished to have exotic reports from the bush. Handwritten. Preferably with a quill, she had said.

Siri is okay, she is. Nags a bit much, but means well. She can laugh at me in a way I can put up with. For Christmas I got a little, beautiful, specially ordered ceramic sign. Not with a name, but with a life motto: "Not my type." "Your type hasn't been invented yet, everyone knows that," she usually says. She can say that sort of thing without it mattering. I laugh myself. But I liked less what she said about initiative. That may have had something to do with its containing a signal about stagnation –

Damn it all!

We passed tents and stands with cloudberry and souvenir sales. It looked as if they weren't selling much. The tourist season was for the most part over.

I neared my goal. Just a few miles more. Very many miles from home. Just that felt good. I had taken off in more than one sense when the plane lifted into the air. At cruising elevation I had been completely euphoric. And felt that this was a feeling that would last.

Maybe she thought she was the one chasing me. That I had enough. But it *was* already enough. More than I could take along. Although in another way. I was full, filled, couldn't take in any more. No, she didn't frighten me. It wasn't *that way*.

"What d'ya want here, really? You're out a little late, you know. They've been here. They've been here, most of them. From Tacitus' envoys on up. *Rio Tinto* and *Se og Hør*, *Norwegian Weekly Journal* and *National Geographic*. We have lots of visitors. She's been here too, Gro.[3] Held a masquerade, – Sami garb and shawl.

And you? Have you gotten a Sami costume?

You haven't. Oh well.

Now we're expecting the Crown Prince himself, the Minister of Commerce. You surely know that there are diamonds here? That there is a bearded half-wit who's been staying up in the mountains for years and scratching and digging, and that he has found some sort of glass pearl now. Maybe that's what you're after – precious stones? Then you're going to be disappointed."

I gave a start. Have to admit it. The tone was … different. Didn't resemble what I had heard up to now. Not that I had had contact with so very many of the young people, but I had exchanged words with a few of them. A couple of them were at the door in the begin-

---

3. Gro Harlem Brundtland. former Prime Minister. Succeeded by the then Minister of Commerce.

ning. Rather persistent. But a little too swaggering and straight to the point for me to have been tempted to let them in.

I had picked up sundry comments, of course – allusions, suggestions, facetious remarks. A little tiring in the long run. But reliable, to be sure. They were boys. Young men, I should perhaps call them. The ones who hang out around the slot-machines and make thousands on Admiral. Or lose.

But this. This was new. I wasn't so naïve that I hadn't expected it. On the contrary – I had expected more. I had been out traveling before. Quite far.

It was the situation, I think. That it was there. In the house I was invited to come to.

"Is that so, you write. Pardon me for saying it, but that's not very original. You do know we're the world's most written about people, don't you? Not so bad to have the world record!

What d'ya say, mamma, aren't you proud?"

The spots that spread out on her throat.

She forgot them behind all the activity. Cups, coffee thermos, ashtrays out – and in again. Some needlework. Always some needlework. Soft leather.

I looked for a balance between staying and going. Helped myself to more coffee. Commented on the sewing. She hadn't intended to use cloth on this purse? No, she answered, she thought this one could be without trim. What did I think? "Fine," I said.

I was in church the first day of Christmas. They were there, the whole family, except him. By whole I mean she herself and the two daughters who were still free as the breeze and had come home for Christmas break to rest up from what they otherwise were busy with and be waited on by a mother who was always there. Was everywhere she was needed. Inside and out, such as mothers are, according to what I've understood.

I had called my own mother the evening before. They were there, everyone. And they thought it was crazy. After all father had offered me money, it wouldn't have cost anything, they could arrange everything from there, send the airplane ticket –

I could hear them in the background. Cackling in unison. Clinking. Uproar. My nieces, in falsetto. My only nephew, in the middle of an aggressive explanation.

I sat on a stool in the hallway of the Mountain Hostel, there was a draft along the floor, the outer door closed and the biting wind came in. It was the manager who came. He shuffled away. On soft shoes. I sat shivering and felt how fine it was to sit precisely there, with the dense darkness outside, the quiet inside. I could taste everything I didn't have to hear: Sniffling, toasts, my sister-in-law's frenetic laughter, the echo from her daughters, mother's detailed and unending descriptions of meals in Rome, Florence "Isn't that right father, it was a delightful time?" And he, with his eyes turned further inward every year. Highballs with the gifts. High praise. Outdo each other with praise. Except for the young, ambitious one. Much too blasé to come out with any shouts. For that matter just as well. But he – deeper and deeper down into the chair. Soon a dot in the pattern. While the lark flitted back and forth. Straightened the tablecloths, fluffed the pillows, filled glasses.

I felt the stiff wind caress my ankles. The cold gust from outside, light and fresh. Nice to breathe in.

They offered me a ride from the church, but I said I had dressed for walking. Had to get a little exercise, and since the weather was so fine –
It was she who was driving. The girl. Slowed and rolled down the window as they drove by.
"Are you sure you don't want to hop in?"
I smiled and waved them away.

Maybe that was wrong?
Maybe my refusal was complete?

In the evening I visited the old woman. It surely sounds stupid, but it felt necessary. I had to go somewhere where I could hold onto the music, or whatever I should call it. The mood from the Christmas service. It stuck. Was engraved with a force I hadn't felt for a long time.
The slow, lingering. That everything was interpreted, and twice as long. The pauses while the other language was heard in the room, but outside of me, past, like pure sound, delay, time. And the hymns, none of them abridged, to the minimum – first and last verse – as I am used to. No, all verses! Slow, swaying, with the organ ahead, the song a notch behind, the familiar tones, and at the same time with something totally unknown to me, as if it were other tones, and yet not.
The church was full. Hot.
And I sat freezing.
Communion finally. One by one they flowed forward from the pews. Without a sound. Filled the circle. Filled it several times.

So that's the way it is?

Not roast turkey with apple.

I had to hold onto it.

Therefore I walked.

They had a Christmas tree in the hallway. That surprised me. I thought they were more orthodox. I mentioned it to one of the nurses I met when I came in.

"No, not here," she said. "Not exactly here with us."

The bed was raised, she was almost sitting. Newly combed. Pretty, I almost said, in a bewildering way. Her skin, so smooth, almost without a trace of time and toil. She was alert, still. Awake and in a good mood.

"A day of joy," she said, "thanks to a good God."

She clapped me on the hand. Wanted to know what I was doing out in the cold, whether I had been to church? I had, I said.

"That's good. Good it is. The one whom the Son gets to redeem, he will be truly free."

She asked what was new. From the village, and from home.

"Have you heard from your family?"

Yes, I surely had.

"And they have peace at Christmas?"

I stayed for quite a while. A young nurse came with coffee and cookies.

I tried them all.

She sat with the same piece of cookie between her fingers the whole time, broke off small bits.

We made small talk about those we both knew. I told about the visit she had, her niece – two of the girls.

She became happy.

"Then they came?"

Then they still find the nest?

It's not worth looking for a strange blessing. Singed wings are all they have."

A tremendous northern light undulated across the sky when I walked back. It billowed wildly, separated into phosphorous green arms, came together, and separated anew. Long tentacles that stretched out.

I had only seen the northern lights a couple of times since I arrived. Then it was thin lights in purple and yellow. It was beautiful.

Now it wasn't.

I was happy when a snowmobile came toward me, with its normal low beams on.

"*Mana dearvan*," she had said when I left. "Fare well."

"And what is it you're writing about?

Is it about the wild barbarians?

In that case, you don't have to strain yourself. You can just make copies of what's been done. There's a bunch, about lice and filth, trash and whores and drinking and destruction. A bunch!

But maybe that's not what you're interested in? Since you roam around up at the rest home. They're probably not very barbaric there. Painstaking work was done. He was satisfied, the head missionary, when he had gotten everyone gagged, burned the art and gotten their hands folded. He was satisfied and you can sure understand that. '*Where the Sami roams he has the book on his chest, God on his lips and Christ in mind.*'

Nicely done.

Are you religious?

I mean, you haven't been sitting up at the rest home for nothing. With our Bible-spouting great aunt. Then it's the noble savage you're chasing after?

Oh well, to each his own.

Maybe it's the blood-curdling story about her daughter you're going to write. The one who had her whole skull bashed in by a much too poorly tamed draft reindeer. You've heard about that, haven't you? Quite a story. It's probably that sort of thing you're out after. Not to mention her husband. That's gotta be food for somebody like you.

You don't have to sit there with a bad conscience.

We're used to it.

We're used to their coming and helping themselves.

And there's still a little left here. For someone really greedy.

Can see you're flushed.

Got a fever or uncomfortable?

Wasn't the coffee any good? I think you drink so little.

You've no doubt gathered that we're a coffee-drinking people? And that we smoke like crazy.

That we drink, you've seen that too of course. Maybe that's your main theme. Your very hypothesis. Nasty stuff.

You've got something there. Absolutely."

She laughed loudly.

It was a sound that pierced.

"You don't say anything.

Not much sound in you.

Oh well, that's fine with me.

There're enough preachers.

Just drink your coffee. Mama'll make more."

Maybe I should have accepted the ride?

I've crossed her path.

Then you don't just walk on.

The next time she came home, the old woman was gone. She was buried right before Easter. She took her leave when they were used to taking leave. When the roads parted, every year. So she remained in practice, carried on what she could.

She wasn't unmoved, the young girl. Didn't hide it either. She took her sister along and visited the grave.

When they got dressed up for the wedding, I saw it too. It couldn't be concealed, either behind noise or humor.

Her mother stood with safety pins in her mouth and put silk on her shoulders. And it wasn't only the silk that was shiny.

Her glance in the mirror before she left.

There was nothing wrong with the edging, it was wide enough, elegant enough. There was nothing wrong with the color on the other costume either. The girls glowed. Their mother had gotten her reward.

I haven't told anyone that she visited me that night.

I had heard the knocking for a while, but didn't attach any importance to it. The night was full of sound. The wedding party was out getting some air. The snowmobiles that took shortcuts over the ground sent flickers of white light into the room, the noise climbed and fell, once in a while you could hear some broken yoik sounds, a car that stopped, doors that slammed, laughter of girls.

It didn't occur to me that the knocking had anything whatsoever to do with me. I lay quietly and let sound and light come and go. Thought: This too I'll take along. A night or two awake is easy to take along for someone on a visit.

What is he doing now, I remember that I thought, – the man with the straight back in the reindeer sled, the one who has stopped dressing up for celebrations? Is he too lying awake during sharp flickers of light? Or has he learned to shut it out?

I think that is precisely what I was thinking about when the energetic knocking began. Four or five minutes passed before I heard steps and the outer door being unlocked. Someone was conversing out there, rather loudly. Then it became quiet again. Until a weak knocking was suddenly heard on my own door.

"Who is it?"

I could hear myself that the voice wasn't steady.

"It's me."

She said her name.

"Can I come in?"

She walked straight and without a sound. Went over and sat down in the only easy chair. Gathered the pleats in the skirt of her costume.

"You don't smoke?"

"Mm, no."

"Oh, well."

She put one foot over the other, swung the tip of her white moccasin, looked around.

"But you can just as well have a smoke," I said, "I can air out afterwards."

She opened the pewter-embroidered purse. Smiled. It struck me that the smiles are extra beautiful on people who are sparing with them. The contrast is staggering. You almost become paralyzed, so strong is the effect.

She had gotten out the pack, Petterøe's blue number three. After having rolled one, she brushed the tobacco particles from her lap and down onto the floor.

"Nice wedding?" I asked. Had to respond to her smile, of course.

I had crept under the covers again. It was cold in the room, and I was thinly dressed in my old, well-used pajamas.

"Well – it was like it usually is. Fun for a while. When they begin to fight, it's not so great. But that would really have been something for you! Loose teeth and blood.

You're missing out on a lot, you've got to figure, when you just lie here.

Alone, even!

So you haven't met anyone?

You've got to work your way in, you see. Get under the skin.

Under the skin!

That was good, wasn't it?"

She laughed. It was a hoarse, joyless laughter. Not derisive.

Sad?

There was something or other fragile about it.

"Participatory observation, it's called. That's what you've got to learn. You can't keep up this sort of thing here – sitting at the rest home and listening to bible verses. Sitting at home with a worn out washwoman and sewing purses! That's something you haven't understood. You get it? Something very basic.

Good grief, lying *here*!

Wha'da you know now? Wha'da you really have to offer?

The apostles' deeds? The aesthetics of purse seams?

Is that anything?

Just admit it – you don't understand anything. So you've hid under the comforter.

Oh well, you aren't the first one who hasn't understood very much. There've been a damn bunch of idiots up here over the years.

But not so many who have lain down. Not that I know. They've wandered around wherever they could get to. And some of them have gotten pretty far. Done it keenly.

But you're cowardly, that's what you are.

Just a big creep, like all the others. But cowardly.

Too bad.

Damn bad.

I've got an article you can borrow. Have it in my apartment, I can send it when I get back. It's in French, you know French? 'Conduites sexuelles dans un groupe de Lapon nomades.' You can read it. Then you'll get some compensation for everything you've missed out on. Maybe you can learn something or other. – Method.

Lie *here*!

Just lie on your back waiting!

Wha'da you got on, by the way? Are those pajamas?

Oh well. They're not very fussy now, everyone. Some people are satisfied with anything.

But don't aim too high. The most deliberate ones aren't so interested in white blood.

Or … wait, of course they screw Norwegian girls too.

But they're careful about not spilling any seeds in them.

Just so you know it."

The cigarette had gone out. She put it down, half-smoked. Began to roll another one. Her fingers wouldn't completely obey her, it was a deformed creature she put between her lips and lit.

"Shit!

Why did I say all that?

Shit!"

She blew smoke toward the ceiling. Closed her eyes. Her arms fell down along the sides of the chair. She was still holding on to the crooked, half destroyed rolled cigarette, twisted it between two fingers. It was the only motion to be picked up.

Several minutes passed. For a while it was so quiet that I could hear the second hand on the alarm clock. It moved rhythmically from point to point on this strange night, which had just now begun to become lighter.

First the smoke fell.

Then she opened her eyes. Bent down and groped on the floor.

Straightened up with a groan. Lighted again.

"I didn't mean …

Really I was going to say that …

I just came to chat, that's really true.

You're actually okay.

Some people go around and ask for a beating, but you …

Damn!

Don't know why I started to talk nonsense.

Typical of me.

Typical, right?"

"Don't worry about it," I said. "It's okay, absolutely okay."

She had put her hat down on the table. Her hair was uncombed. The fringes on the shawl slid out of her neckline, a sparse cluster that spread in all directions. She seemed a little lost sitting there, with the silk shawl lopsided. Disheveled.

"Would you … would you like a glass of beer?"

She looked up. Surprised.

I got two. Opened them. Handed her one.

I couldn't really know that it was too much.

I got up. Put my arms around her.

Or was it she who put her arms around me.

I'm not certain.

It was morning when she left. She took the short cut over the meadow. The crust was hard after the night, supported her.

She looked so light. Her gait was light. Her purse swung. Her skirt swung. A morning bird, one of the most colorful, over the white crust.

I couldn't know that it was a mistake.

Again.

Like that time, with the old woman.

I'm bringing something with me.

That's enough. The presence. That's enough.

You wouldn't have believed there was so much weighing her down.

Such light steps over the crust.

But they were there. On her silk shoulders. Everyone.

She asked whether I had lost anyone.
I said I had.

A little nod. Alert.

They were five siblings, she said. No age difference to speak about, they had come one after the other.

She remembers the warmth of the others when they sat on the snowmobile sled. Father was steering, mother sitting in back. It was an Okkelbo they had, one of the first snowmobiles that arrived.

Just like that it happened that one of them tumbled off and rolled along in the snow. While the others laughed. Father most of all. Mother brushed the snow off and nudged the unlucky one in place again, scolded them all and asked them to hold onto each other, hold on properly, hold on firmly.

"I have two brothers," she said.
"One of them wears a suit, the other's a drunk.
We've lost them both."

But it was when she spoke about the one who was swept away by white blood that I had to get up and put my arms around her.

Much is hazy from that night.

I think I lost the train of thought.

After we had rocked each other, as if we were each other's children, she continued to speak, in a steady voice now, a new peace.

While I was stuck. Stuck in all the suits they wear, my own family. My brother. Tons of suits. Father. His look steadily deeper inward. Into his silence. His sedated silence. I was stuck in the fragrance of perfume and in an empty room.

Backs moving away.

There wasn't bitterness in what she told. At any rate, not against me, that I could notice.

She explained, calmly like an old, experienced teacher, one who doesn't have to emphasize, one who is self-confident in what he does, and more tolerant than most others. Patiently she explained.

She went far back. Knew the lines. Accounted for everything that was taken – bit by bit. Something about plunder and something about cunning. When they took the river, they had with them an army in uniform. She had been too little to be there. Her brother, the oldest, had been old enough. But he turned away. Has always done that. Ever since he was in primary school and had good manners shaken into his body. The Norwegian teachers called it that: Good manners. That meant that he was supposed to hang his down jacket on a peg. At home there were other things that counted. But it was the pegs that were in force. All the pegs.

Her sisters mostly look down. I've seen them, haven't I? They walk around pawing and scraping. Have become so small that they can be crushed between the fingertips, like mosquitoes, or flies.

It's tough.

She ascertained.

Tough to put up with when you've been trained to stand with your hat in your hand.

Getting rid of it is an effort.

She has tried. Tries.

She has run into most everything. The half-hearted good will is worst. Unwieldy. A tough shell that only gets thicker if you tug at it.

I felt that she was observing me. That she couldn't be sure. Of course, you can never be completely sure.

Presumably she noticed my unease. Said:

"At any rate you don't wear the costume. That's a plus. You don't put on the costume."

I couldn't tell whether her mildness was pure exhaustion after a long night.

Perhaps it was trust.

Perhaps a test.

I fell asleep not long before day. My body was all keyed up. It trembled.

I didn't get up properly until the day after. Went out to the café and bought myself breakfast. I had to get away from the cramped room. There was too much in the walls that couldn't be aired out.

It was teeming in the café, clatter and uproar and I don't know how many languages. A couple of Germans in silver-colored snowmobile suits drowned out the rest who turned into a steady roar, a sound tapestry that settled around me, deadened my heartbeats, soothed my blood that was pumping so very fast. I turned my back when an American in a good frame of mind began to wave a telephoto lens in all directions, I had accidentally put myself in focus, under an impressive antler crown. He shouted to me, wanted me to look at him with a toothy smile beneath the antlers. He wanted a little boy in his Sunday best to sit on the lap of his ample wife. He got neither and became irritated.

Afterwards I got dressed, took out the skis, put on a layer of red/blue wax under the middle and set out.

I found a trail that swerved off from the staked-out snowmobile track. In a short time I was beyond the engine roar, outside the range of the lenses.

I wasn't high. Yet above most. The landscape was gentle – hill upon hill endlessly inwards.

On the second rise I sat down, laid the skis nicely on edge, laid mittens and scarf under my seat.

So easy it had been to get there!

A few plants of the poles. Then I was there.

Could have been there before. Many times.

I had narrowed the radius myself. Had no one to blame. Something was beginning to oppress.

She had cited one prophet or another. It must have been a ways into the night. After what she said about them not spilling their seeds in just anyone.

His name was Turi, I think.

It was something about being able to live up high – live out your thoughts there. In the dense forest, he had said, the Sami couldn't think clearly. But if the meetings had been held on the high mountain, then he would have managed to explain everything.

That occurred to me where I was sitting. Cold in my seat, but with my eyes freer than in a long time.

More occurred to me.

It occurred to me what she had said about steeling herself:

"You have to be so invulnerable that you can cut yourself with the knife without bleeding."

You know how they hardened themselves in the old days, she asked me.

"No."

"They boiled lye from ashes and drank it. The *noaides*[4] did it."

No, lye I had never drunk.

Nor she, I think.

---

4. Shamans.

It was chock-full in the Sports Hall. Gore-Tex and silk, parkas and party garb, ski boots and soft moccasins. The entire hall was thick with signs. Some of them I could make out. Innocence tramped in on ornamented ski boots, untouched as if before the fall of man. Stretched his arms out to the sides and grabbed five chair backs at the same time, reserved a spot for his group. Naturalized Norwegian immigrants with factory-made Sami boots on their feet. Somewhat more hesitant in the competition for the empty seats.

I had come early, found a seat about in the middle, stayed there.

I saw that they came in. They came together, the sisters. New costumes on. Not too much yellow, not too much green, nor pretentious white.

I sat and pondered colors.

I had learned!

I sat with childlike delight and let my eyes roam.

The musicians tuned their instruments. Hectic around the stage, many working. Light master, technicians of various sorts, all with their specific tasks. Wordless instructions, elements that fell into place, little by little, where they were supposed to be.

That's the way it must have been around the tents. That's roughly the way they had described it, both – the one who always sews and her recently buried godmother. Everything fell quietly into place. No orders. The knowledge was there. When they pitched camp, they just had to bring it about. The herd grazing, the canvas over the slender poles, birch twigs on soft snow, a layer of plump hides, furthest inside the tent the chest with food, an armful of wood inside the door.

The curtain is tested, the instrument cases put away. Everything ready. The light master has his area under control. The spotlights are where they are supposed to be. The sound is modulated from the mixing desk not far from where I am sitting. The music is alternately new and old. Very old. The scale is pentatonic, I have read. That is supposed to be a very archaic feature. The tones are hurled out and die away, are hurled out again, glide over peaks, unfamiliar territory, glide away and come back. They go in circles, I know, but don't hear it.

My ear doesn't hear.

Maybe it's that way with everything? That it has its scale. One that my ear can't reach –

What about my eyes?

Recently I sat in innocent peace and thought I could ponder colors.

Flowers and applause.

Then an uneven stream out into the frosty evening.

She sees me, and doesn't see me.

Finds her flock.

The points I walk between become steadily fewer.

I feel frozen, in the mild weather. Frozen even though my fingers are clammy inside the wool mittens.

Those I meet, see me, and see that it is a stranger walking. Things haven't changed much. On the contrary, it has gotten stronger. I feel like hiding myself in a wide street. Going into a café. Sitting for a long time with a cup of coffee and being invisible.

Here, in this light, even my gray mittens are garish.

It was her mother who had asked me to come.

I found an occasion to comment on it, so that she heard, the youngest daughter, where she was scurrying zealously here and there, back and forth and out into the hallway. There she set herself up and shouted into the telephone.

Her mother poured coffee.

The other daughter came with knife and dried meat.

Was this what the student called pawing and scraping?

I ate. It was good. Salty and good.

My older friend didn't want any. This was the third year they had dried meat from reindeer they hadn't slaughtered themselves.

"You eat," she said, "eat!"

"Well, how is your research going?" the girl interrupted.

"You're good at sneaking around. I saw you were at the concert. Will say that you were forbidding sitting there, with camera and whatever else hanging on you. You were lacking only a pith helmet.

Wha'da you think of the music? Nice with bongo drums, isn't it?"

I wasn't quick enough, as usual. She heard my stammering before I'd had time to open my mouth.

She had several errands on the telephone.

Errands here and there. Quickly over.

Many lively friends on the telephone.

I wasn't able to console her perplexed mother with the fact that I knew another side. Then I would have betrayed the nocturnal visit – that she presumably would like to have undone.

I had bribed her with a bottle of beer.

Now she had to get something back.

She had given me her dreams.

That's too much.

In one dream everyone was there. Her four siblings, children still, small and quick, running in all directions, into narrow streets, out into another block, into other narrow streets, between cars on the move, into alleys, dark alleys with threatening shapes leaning against walls, tapping feet, further, always further. And their mother after, hurrying after them, but doesn't catch up, slides into a plastic cloth, a blue plastic cloth, slides under, it melts, she stays there, waves her arms, but the cloth only closes tighter around her. And she, the fifth one, shouts, shouts to their father on the other side of the wide square, but he doesn't hear, he is there, but can't hear, her voice doesn't carry, it is too weak in the din, doesn't carry. They are gone, all four are gone into the streets, their mother under blue plastic, their father in the shadow of the wall.

In the second dream there is just one.

He is the one she has wasted way too many years on.

The one who didn't wait.
The one who married white blood.

He comes driving along the river. She stands waiting. It is dark, she can't see contours, just sees the light, the sharp light from the snow-mobile, it flutters weakly, up and down, the river ice is uneven, the light dances in step with the rough surface.

Suddenly the light is gone.

No sound. No shout.

She tries to place one foot in front of the other, but the foot doesn't want to obey, it turns aside, is forced back.

She stands there silent and stiff.

Knows that the light disappeared into an open channel.

So much, and more, for a beer.
A whole world for a bag of glass pearls.

Not even then, when she mentioned her father and his deal – a high price for a deleted earmark – not even then did I say anything.

"Do you know what it means to be no one?" she asked.

I didn't find the words, otherwise I could have mentioned the silence I know about. The one that came after all the young men with welted shoes and squeaking pagers.

I could have mentioned the glance turned inward. The chair becoming steadily deeper. The lark's song – more and more stridently false.

A slow, gentle fall.

I didn't find the words?

Or didn't I want to find them?

Was I walking into a tradition?

She had come home on vacation that time too.

The whole village was looking forward to seeing the expression on her face.

But she was ready.

Her mother had called when it began to become public. When there had been more than a few visits.

He had begun to stay there, with the new teacher, a woman, day after day. His car boldly outside.

She was prepared. No one was going to see her bent over.

They didn't either.

She had partied a bit with her brother then. He was still at home. They were a whole gang. Had enough to drink. One of them had a camera.

It was three years ago.

Exactly.

She changed her place of study after that. Couldn't get far enough away.

Now she was on the telephone.

Was still standing there when I left. Didn't raise her eyes.

I was without contours, invisible.

The swans had arrived when I left. I caught a glimpse of them from the bus. Three of them bobbing in a narrow ice channel. They need so little. Six inches deep is enough – down to the bottom. Some lakes have two bottoms. Saivo is the name of the land that lies furthest down. It is an ideal world. The gods live there.

But the swans swim above. In small circles. They didn't have time to wait.

The snow sparrow had already been there for several weeks. Didn't have time to wait either. Came with small wing beats, in graceful formations through the air.

"They're out early, poor creatures. The winter winds are still blowing."

She had seen them, the busy one.
Between all the work periods.

I was headed in the opposite direction.
It felt too early, that too.
And about time.

My colleagues ask questions. I find that entirely reasonable.
Then I mention the official report that still isn't finished.

Minerals for example are not a completely trivial question.

Or I say something about the language situation – that there is will, basically, in name anyway, but that the appropriations are meager.

I say that the readjustment program for reindeer operations – getting herders out of the business because of overgrazing – is not very satisfactory. There is no alternative. Far too many who are switched over to welfare.

They shrug their shoulders. Say they can read too.

They inquire less often now.

At home things are about the same. I don't think there is any change of note.

But it *feels* different.

I go there more often.

See that it makes them happy.

Mother doesn't twitter quite so loudly.

Always when I walk past the chest of drawers with the mirror in the hall on the way out, I can notice a special fragrance. It comes from the flask that used to stand there long, long ago. A dark perfume bottle with pink tassels. When they were going out, she always stopped there, lifted the flask up, a final spray behind the ears. First one, then the other.

The fragrance was still there after they had gone.

My brother used to misbehave. Had to get a swat from the babysitter.

While I sat completely still and enjoyed the fine fragrance.

I can still sense it.

She called me at work. I was quite taken aback.

"Hi, it's me."

Whether I had time? Interested? Whether we could maybe meet some day?

There are two images that are clearer than the others.

One is of the light steps over the crusty snow. Fluttering hem on her costume. A beautiful image. Entirely false.

The other is the throng after the concert. She is there and she isn't. Impossible to reach.

Meet?

It feels like I have something to atone for.

I'm there first. Take one of the empty tables outside. Perhaps there was a thought there, far back, that it might be nice with open sky, air.

The waiter is on the spot. I ask to wait with the order. He dances on.

Then I catch sight of her. She is close by. Dressed in light colors, small and with the smooth, blond hair swinging down toward her shoulders.

Had I expected her to stand out? I had had my eyes far away.

Gracefully picks her way between the chairs and is there.

"Bures."

She stretches her hand out.

I take it and smile in reply.

She slides down, squints against the sun.

"Maybe you wanted to sit inside?" I ask.

"No. No, it's nice here. I haven't gotten very much sun lately." She straightens her back, lifts her pale face so the sun can shine into it and smooth out what had to be there from the stress of exams.

I wave to the waiter.

"Beer," she says. And grins.

"Beer for me too, please."

There is a sudden ease in the air, which makes me giggle. I am eighteen years old and ordering my first beer in a café.

The waiter is back quickly with a fully loaded tray. We each get our ice cold, foamy glass.

"Skål."

"Máiste."

Two sharp sounds when the glasses are put down on the marble top again. A young man bumps into my chair on his way past. I flinch. A sudden trembling in my chest.

I try to pick up the thread. Pick up one that isn't too fragile.

"You had exams?"

"Yes."

"And it went well?"

"Think so. The grading is next week. And orals."

A completely unnecessary warning light. Her voice is firm and mild.

"Thought you had certain reservations about social anthropology," I joke.

She laughs loudly. Not at all jarring.

"Surely you know how to put out a grass fire?"

I have some idea, I answer.

She is a playful hare, jumps over everything that has been said before.

Can this be the same girl?

The bitterness, the wariness – blown away!

Was it the exam that worried her?

Or does everything have to do with time and space?

It is almost just the handbag that is the same. And the tobacco pack.

I ask what kind of plans she has down the road and she says that she will begin on a major in the fall.

"Can you guess what I am planning to specialize in?"

"No idea."

"Norwegian culture."

She serves it up with a sharp u and final stress.

"Alright!"

She pauses deliberately, stretches her neck, looks out into the air, mysteriously, her eyes are wily crevices. She is bubbling.

The tables around us fill up. A sunburned and long limbed girl asks whether she can take one of our chairs.

My friend makes a friendly sign with an open hand.

"Is that so. Norwegian culture. And what'll it be about? Have you found out what it is?"

"Yup."

"Well?"

"The essence of Norwegian culture," she begins, slowly, elaborately, "the crux if you will, there are three things."

"Yeah?"

"The first is snow shoveling."

I assume a serious expression, nod solemnly.

"And the second?"

"The second is eating potatoes."

The solemn expression doesn't hold. Not with her either, we break into laughter, lean over the table and shake. People turn around, with indulgent glances. Hysterical, they probably think. They cannot know that what they see is the dew vanishing before the sun, a new and playful feather under the chin, a grass fire being put out.

I control myself, put on a normal expression, take a swallow.

"And the third?"

"The third is the perpetual complaining about the economy."

I can't remember the last time I was in such an elevated mood.

We order food.

She asks for an extra helping of potatoes for me.

People around us come and go. We sit. The sun has lost its grip, it has suddenly gotten cooler.

When I asked her whether she hadn't forgotten any points, a fourth and a fifth – the tendency to sniff around and to instruct, she became objective. Answered that it wasn't specifically enough Norwegian. The European splinter in the eye was more general than that.

I was glad she stopped there. For a moment I was afraid I had started something more. That had occurred to me already when she called. Now she's got me, I thought. Now she's circled me in, been to the library, counted the average number of stereotypes per page in my big Africa tome. I got ready for a left hook, an uppercut, a straight right. Knew it was coming. My body resisted. Had I been an animal with fur, it would have been visible.

But it didn't come.

She stopped there. As if in a sort of agreement.

The food had settled in our bodies. Only good will and sauce remnants left. The waiter cleared the table.

"Very nice here," she says.

She is looking out over the fjord, in toward the harbor, out again.

A passenger ship has just shoved off from the pier, glides past.

Akershus castle looms straight ahead.

"Quite a structure," she comments. Nods toward the portal to the land.

Sea wall. Earthwork. Defense.

No more than that: "Quite a structure."

We sit for a while without saying anything.

I feel an almost overwhelming happiness that it is possible. Her mother and I could be silent together. For a long time. While she sewed. Or walked to and fro. I could sit without being on the verge of doing anything.

Much more uneasy at home with my own family. Sharper sounds there. Sudden shifts.

In the course of my stay up there she took me along on a shopping trip to the innermost part of the fjord a couple of times. Then we were silent. The whole way. While the road markers swept past. Bogs and dwarf birch, low mountain hills, frozen lakes, ice sheets hanging out over the crags, green and glistening.

She slowed down where there was a danger of reindeer, otherwise she kept up a steady speed, her eyes calmly ahead.

It was on Saturdays we went, when she didn't have any washing.

When we arrived at the cabin area with smoke from the chimneys, parked cars, snowmobiles on the ice, she had a ready commentary.

"Just think that they want to live this way. When they have electricity and running water at home!"

She shook her head.

It was never oppressive to be silent.

Nor is it now.

She didn't have a particular errand. And I don't ask whether anyone has sent her.

We both know that our meeting will soon be over. That we will each go our own way.

She will go home. I haven't asked, but know it. She'll go home, both now and later on.

There are so few left who care, she said, that night. So few left.

She had planned and conducted a seminar then.

All the noisy telephone conversations.

The wall of sound and laughter.

I am no longer invisible, so I plunge ahead, inquire. She shrugs her shoulders. It had gone fairly well, you know. Not all that many showed up. To put it mildly.

No, they have crept into the sofa nooks, the ones whom she worked with before in the association. There they sit enjoying themselves, study car brochures. That'll soon be the only thing they study – brochures!

She reminds me mostly of a tired soldier sitting there. Dressed in summer white, as if straight from the desert. On leave. Pause in the war. Sweaty brow and fresh beer.

It is the direction that has gone away, she explains to me.

For a while it was there. But now it is exactly as if it goes around in circles. When something is reached, big or small, it is as if the air goes out, it gets quiet. Everything becomes insipid.

"Let the devil take the heat when the others just give up.

The hell with them!"

She probably shouldn't blame them for that, she says. Understands them, really. Over and over again the same thing. And to what use? When they have gotten a ways, everything begins anew. New government, new greenhorns in all positions, centrally, locally, begin from scratch, explain, after a while think that now, now there is something that is understood, has permeated, fallen into place, an insight, an agreement, a beginning.

And then it is finished.

Again.

The soldier has seen more. Eaten from the tree of knowledge.
That was strong fare, burns in the body.
Nothing better to carry than knowledge, they say.
An insult to them who bear it.

Now the soldier rests. Eyes on the approach to the city they say no
one leaves without being hurt.

Maybe she has drunk lye after all.

I rush right on.

I shouldn't have done it.

She should have had peace.

Yes, he had visited her, her older brother. That never happened before. It has always been she looking for him.

He was exhausted, worn out. She prepared food, but he didn't eat much. She made a bed on the sofa. He lay down, but couldn't sleep. Lay there and smoked and stared at the ceiling. There wasn't much talk in him, but he said he intended to go home. She promised to help him with the ticket. She was so relieved. Thought that everything would finally turn out well. Better. So much easier now, when nothing is waiting. Everything was finished. Settled. Load after load driven to the slaughterhouse. The cabin torn down. Yeah, the latter was unnecessary. They could have had it. They'd wanted to keep it, the others. It was that way. But he had taken along a crow bar, father, big as a bear spear, tore it down and leveled it, didn't stop until he was finished.

I don't ask what he intends to do there. Whether there is work. Whether he is just going to go there and turn right around.

The migratory birds leave when they have to. Isn't always so much to leave for.

An open channel in the ice. Six inches deep. You have to keep moving in order not to freeze solid.

That he can do.

That he has probably always done. A wild man up along the river on unsafe ice, clenched fists into the wall, kicking the door.

As if he knew that it would be too crowded, you had to break free.

This I know from the night she visited me.

She told me about the siblings. Who had gone away.

One behind all the city's roofs.

The other behind an answering machine.

Her sisters who bite the dust.

One in a discount store.

The other with no salary.

And she herself?

In open air, hovering between many rooms, equally unfamiliar in all.

The best moments are when she is packing for a trip, she said.

Whether in one direction or the other.

The fever-ridden boy from the river.

The serious herder on his father's lap.

The school boy with his jacket on the peg.

He's going home.

Me with all my practical deliberations – work or no work, house or no house.

Naturally he is going to leave.

When he can.

She got so happy, the old one, when I said that the girls had come.

So relieved she was that they had found the nest.

It isn't much of the Sami language I've managed to learn.

I know that *ruoktu* means home. And that *ruoktot* means back.

"That's nice," I say.
To say something.
She shakes her head.
So there is more.

She had needed peace. This short while.
Again I.
Like a vulture after open wounds.

"Where there is no wound, the blood doesn't run either."

"He disappeared."
She looks down. "Again," she adds.
Has she looked?
"Hm ... Everywhere."

I remember a tale I read while I was up there. It was about what they call the Barbmo kingdom:

In the autumn all the birds left and went to the Barbmo kingdom. Some tiny people lived there who were called the Barbmo kingdom people. They were no larger than swans, but they hunted both geese and other kinds of birds. They had a long pole, and at the end of the pole they had a snare. They managed to slip it over the neck of the bird, and that way they strangled it. They ate very carefully, without breaking a bone. Afterwards they collected the bones and brought them to the place where they had caught the bird.

One time two brothers came to the Barbmo kingdom people and got to see how they hunted. They noticed that the birds didn't seem to be the least bit afraid of these people.

The brothers stayed there for a spell while they studied their secret customs in hiding. They saw that when the people cleaned a goose or another bird, they were very careful not to break the bones. And when they had cooked the meat, they saw how they ate so that the bones would remain just as whole.

The brothers were also invited to a meal. They did the same thing. They ate very carefully and gathered the bones together when they were finished. The people liked that a lot, they understood.

When they had eaten, everyone took each other by the hand and gave thanks.

The brothers as well.

Then they gathered the bones in a vessel, and one person carried them over to the place where the bird was caught.

The people in the Barbmo kingdom tried to convince the brothers to stay longer with them.

But that they didn't want.

"What about you?"

She has livened up. I ordered coffee. She recovered quickly. She is used to suffering, gets tired, rests – and gets up. Used to being knocked to the ground – and going on.

"Well ..."

"Talk now. What were you really doing up there?"

"Well, I ..."

"Did you find a little niche, something you can convert? Or was it a so-called adventure journey you were on – a year among the Lapps, the simple, primitive life, the pact with nature and that sort?"

"Something like that."

"You seemed a little frightened, in a way. Almost as if you were running away –"

It comes without a side-glance, without an obvious joker up the sleeve or a cold shower.

"Maybe the book was just an excuse to get away?"

She comes straight at me, and this time I find words. About it being too painful to be in the slow fall. That I had an idea about something entirely different, something easier. High heaven and high mountain plateaus were the easiest thing I managed to picture before me.

Like an image, to step into. Alone.

She doesn't even smile.

Nor ask whether there was more.

She knows it.

The book was real enough. It was supposed to deal with structures.
What I was trained to look for.

But the lines disappeared, they vanished.

A system requires distance.

I got too close.

"It'll appear … in time?"

She sounds like someone consoling.

"Hardly."

"I … was … pretty mean, huh?"

There is no triumph in this voice.

Then she has taken it with her.

Taken even more on her silk shoulders.

I laugh it away. Say I learned a saying from her mother.

"Let me hear."

"An old dog can bite a thicker leash."

She smiles. Pours more coffee. Pours for me too.

"Just drink your coffee. Mamma'll make some more."

Transformation?

No one likes to display their distress.

I try to imagine a stranger in the large living room with lark
chirping and the disappearing dot in the chair.

"You … so … I probably exaggerated a little."

"Concerning?"

"About aiming high."

I think she is blushing. If barely.

"Really?"

"It was no doubt pure wishful thinking," she giggles. "Back to the eighties, or something like that. If not the seventies."

"Oh darn. Did I miss out on a lot, do you think?"

"You bet!"

We stop there. In a liberating laughter. Stop before we reach open channels, white blood. Or the empty rooms after everything I have let pass.

We have an agreement about how far we go.

As if we have gone on trips together before and have a regular place to rest, take our skis off, lay mittens and scarf under our seats.

Music is coming from the restaurant boat lying moored a bit away.

She listens to the music, swings her one foot.

Without closing my eyes I call forth the image of the white moccasin tip.

While the sandal foot continues to swing, gently.

I call forth the image of the man on the sofa too.

With the foot sliding. And being put in place.

So quiet it can be.

So completely calm.

The young girl is right that I am cowardly.

Afraid of remaining in the fragrance. Staring at the flask. Listening for doors that slam.

You should have been bold. Let yourself be lifted by the eagle talons.

"So it wasn't a diamond hunt you were on then?"

I hem and haw. "Yes. In a sense."

"Did you find any?"

"A whole sack."

"Fine. Then you are rich now?"

"Yes."

"Good."

She sits leaning back in the straight chair. It has steel tubing, is neither deep nor soft, but she seems to be sitting well. When I see her thus, half in profile, I see who she resembles. In the light blouse and with the lines smoothed out in her face, as now, after hours of squinting in the sun, she reminds me of the old woman. It is the same glance, sharp and mild at the same time. It has a jarring radiance, and you have the feeling that it is boring through you and moving on, moving past everything that refracted it. That it rests on a point far out. On a mirage, or dream.

She appears clearly again, the old woman.

Newly combed, serene, on the white pillow.

After having fought.

Above the headboard – the man on Nebo.

Looking out.

We get up, as if on signal.

Accompany each other along the wharf over to the bus stop.

The sun is shining low now. The city hall clock shows almost nine.

She swings up the step and into the bus.

At the same time as she sits down and turns her face toward me to wave, my reflection merges with her image, behind the glass, becomes entirely one – forehead, eyes, chin. It is unclear where she begins and I end, just a weak film between, like a reflection on a badly adjusted TV, a flickering contour.

It only lasts a moment, but long enough for me to become bewildered. My hand stops on the way up. I was going to wave, but can't wave at my own mirror image.

The bus starts in motion, and the images drift apart from each other. It happens so fast. I barely manage to get my hand up.

Then she is gone.